Diabolic Angel

SANDRA MOLES

Contents

Wings

- -

I woke up refreshed and happy. That was seriously the best sleep I have had in a long time, I thought to myself, as I sat up in the bed and stretched. I looked at the clock and smiled. It was 10:57 a.m. Huh, I slept over fourteen hours.

I threw the covers off and walked over to the mirror across the room. I closed my eyes and took a deep breath and willed them to appeared. It took a minute for them pop out. When I opened my eyes, there they were: my wings. They were so beautiful and majestic. I smiled.

I stood a certain way to where I could only see one of my wings. Black is such a pretty color, I thought to myself, as I touched the feathers. They were so soft.

You see, before I was even born, the fates had foretold the destiny of the world. It was written that two angels would get together and have a child, which nowhere in the Bible is there record of a child being born from two angels. So, what do you call a child who is born from two angels? Apparently, I am called an Empyrean. I am a heavenly being, although I do not feel heavenly. I still feel normal. I am normal looking besides these wings protruding from my back. My hair is about an inch or two past my shoulders that I dyed black shortly after my parents died. I am five feet eight inches tall, with a medium build. I weigh 145 pounds and I have been told that I am a big ball of fury, when provoked.

I laugh as I remember how much my life has changed in the past week. Millenniums ago, my entire life was basically already written. A child so pure was going to be born, the time unknown, according to records. They had said that both good and evil would seek out this child and basically try to convince the child to choose their side. That child was me. I had to choose between Heaven and Hell, good and evil. I was predicted to be the world's savior or the world's destruction. That is such a big choice for a not-yet seventeen-year-old to make. To top that choice off, I had to decide all of this before the time I was born; before my seventeenth birthday. I decided the fate of the world two days ago.

It's amazing when I take the time to think about it. Up until a week ago, I believed that if I couldn't see something, it meant that it didn't exist. Boy, was I wrong. Well, when I met Lucifer, that all changed, my beliefs and my life. I found out a week ago that Lucifer marked me when I was six, the same day that my parents died, marking me to rule aside him, if I chose him and his evil side.

I didn't want to accept that there was another world around me. I would get terrible headaches, which I found out was sort of like a third vision, you know, I was able to see a whole other world coexisting with humans around me. The more I fought it and denied myself the truth, the worse it got. However, there was no denying that there was another world when I was kidnapped by the ruler of Hell, Lucifer.

I spent ten years alone with no one to love or care about me but my protector, Micheal Angelo. I didn't, however find out that Micheal wasn't human until five minutes before my birthday. When Lucifer joined my life a week ago, he threw it into a chaotic order. Then, before my birthday after I found out about everything, proving my whole life was a lie, I threw myself off the highest building in our little town. I mean, how do you choose between the person you grew up with and the person you were destined to be with?

Now that I have made the choice of the world, I must live with it. If anyone was to ask me, 'do I regret making the choice I made?' I would tell them no. Every choice I have ever made in my life, has had supporting reasons behind it. I made my choice, deciding the fate of the world for a reason. There is nothing in this world that would change my choice.

"Man," a voice, that I was all too familiar with, sighed, "so much has changed in the last week, huh?" I turned to face Lucifer and he smiled at me.

"You can say that again," I laughed as I punched him on the shoulder. He was responsible for over half the changes in my life. Without him and Micheal, I would be living a 'normal' life. Lucifer fingered the feather on my wings, causing me to shudder. I could feel every little touch he made. "So pretty," he complimented.

"I know," I said, smiling. "Who knew that I was an angel?"

"I did," Lucifer raised his hand.

"Shut-up." I rolled my eyes at him and sighed. "What is on today's agenda?"

"Well, nothing much, my Angel. I thought we could start the day off by either getting you educated on defending yourself or spending the day getting you introduced to the people, demons, souls, and tortured," Lucifer said.

I scrunched my nose up. "Is there anything else we can do instead?"

"We could always get to know each other, if you wish. I know my bed has been missing some action, lately." Lucifer wiggled his eyebrows.

"Ew! Gross! No!" I grimaced.

"Have you had your sheets cleaned recently?"

"Yes. My servants clean them every day. What do you choose Raven?" Lucifer asked.

"I think I'll choose fighting," I said. "I mean I need to know how to defend myself if someone tries to kill me again. "

"That is so true. But are you sure you don't want to save fighting for another day?"

"No. I want to do it now. Every second I put off learning to fight, means that every second I put myself in danger of being injured or attacked," I pointed out, crossing my arms.

Lucifer shrugged and said, "It's your choice. Come on. I figured you would want to fight so I had the staff build me a training center next to the mansion. Let's go before the demons start hunting. Just because you are with me, does not mean that the demons know that you are off limits. They created this tradition where they feed on the damned down here."

I swallowed and asked, "How do we let the demons know that I am not to be...hunted?"

"Oh, that is easy. I will be holding a ball."

"Oh, okay." I didn't know how to dance so this should be fun. Plus, this would be my first ball. I have learned when it comes to Lucifer, don't argue, he doesn't change his mind easily.

"Let's go, now." Lucifer grabbed my hand, leading me out of the room. Watch your wings on the door."

I nodded as I followed him. Before I left the room, I gave a second glance at the mirror behind me. They were both so pretty: my black and white wings.

Kharon

"One more time," Lucifer yelled from across the room. "This time, remember your form, Angel! Also, don't worry about hurting Caleb, Raven. He's a demon after all. If he can survive undergoing a demon transformation, then she can survive fighting you."

Sighing, I walked over to the wall that held the weapons that Lucifer was allowing me to fight with. I picked up something that was called a Katondra. It was like a multi-purpose sword. If you press the button at the top of the sword, the blade pops out. If you slide down the button on the side, then it turns into a tazor. When neither of the items were activated, it was simply a staff, that was how I have been using it.

"Wait for my signal," Lucifer instructed. "Ready...set...fight!" he yelled as the bell rang.

I could see that Caleb was waiting for me to make the first move. It would be easier to fight him with my wings but they fucking dissapear. Cowards!

Sighing, I thought, Here goes nothing. I took a deep breath and did my best warrior cry as I took off towards Caleb, with my Katondra raised. I swung my Katondra at Caleb, who dodged my swing. He swung at me and I didn't move in time and his fist hit me on the side of my face. "Shit!"

I whispered, as I grimaced. I tried to call for a time out, but Caleb swung at me again knocking me to the ground.

I cried out, as I hit my head on the ground. A little dazed, I scurried out of the way of Caleb's foot. I barely made it out of the way as his foot hit the ground with a thud.

He is not going to go easy on me. I need to find his weakness. He has one, right? That was when I got an idea in my head. I kicked him in the shin, hard. I heard a crack as he fell to the ground.

I laughed as I stood up. "Good job, Raven," Lucifer praised. I looked over at him and smiled. "Watch-"

I swung my head around too late as Caleb struck me with his Katondra. I groaned as the electric current ran through my body. When he pulled his weapon away, I dropped my Katondra and fell to the ground. I gasped, trying to calm my heart rate.

Shit, that hurt like a bitch! I looked up just in time to see Caleb going for another blow. I rolled to this to dodge his hit. Without thinking, I swung both of my feet around and kicked Caleb in the back of his legs, causing his to basically fold like a sheet. When he dropped his Katondra, I snatched it up and slid both buttons, on the weapons. I placed one foot on his chest, keeping him pinned to the ground. I growled as the weapon started to spark. He's going to pay!

Right as I was about to strike him with both weapons, Caleb held his hands out, in front of his face. "I call a withdraw. I'm done."

Rolling my eyes, I shut down the weapons and let him up. "You're a loser," I said.

"I can beat your butt, Raven, I just don't want to damage you," Caleb came back at me. "Besides, I am a demon. I am practically invincible."

From across the room, Lucifer clapped his hands, slowly. "Good job, Raven. I am impressed. Your form was pretty good. It could use some improvement but pretty good overall. I think that is all we are going to do today. You will have more training, later with someone else. Caleb, I think it is time for you all to go feed."

Caleb smiled, showing his sharp demon teeth. "Fuck yeah!" he yelled as he took off.

"Come on, Raven. I want to show you something," Lucifer said, grabbing my hand.

"Where are we going?" I asked while I followed him.

"I want to show you to the beginning to all this Hell," he grinned at me.

"Before we meet Kharon, I want to warn you, some people say that he is super scary. Do not shake his hand." Lucifer warned as we walked to the gates of Hell.

"Okay, whatever," I said, rolling my eyes. I was starting to think that everyone down here was super scary and would disintegrate me by a meer touch.

Lucifer walked up to a clocked figure, who was standing by two Iron poles. Lucifer tapped the figure on the back. "Raven, I want you to mean Kharon. Kharon, this is Raven," Lucifer introduced me to a tall, slender man. This guy had pitch black hair and white eyes. At first, I was taken back by his looks, but when he spoke, that all changed.

"Nice to meet you ma'aam," Kharon said in a think county accent. "Welcome to the most pleasant place on Earth where the rides are free and screams are welcomed."

I burst out laughing when I heard him speak. "You're country? You are not scary at all!" I laughed. "In fact you are kind of cute." I bit my lip as I looked him up and down. I mean, besides his white eyes, he was pretty cute in a geeky way. Way too skinny for my taste, though.

"He's not that cute, Raven," Lucifer mumbled.

"Why are your eyes white?" I asked.

"It allows me to see anywhere in the world at any time. For example, I can see that that portal is about to open in three, two, one."

"Raven, you might want to step back," Lucifer advised a portal manifested between the two iron poles.

Kharon grew three feet and he growled as he bent over, in I guess pain. When he stood back up I could see his appearance had completely changed. His skin had shrunk into his face making the veins in his face pop out. His skin turned an ashen grey with splotches of black. Two black holes stood in the place of where his white eyes once were. The skin around his mouth was no more, showing pointy teeth.

I gasped as the once cute boy was no longer catching my attention. "Think he's cute now?" Lucifer asked with a smirk.

"Fuck you," I hissed, as I watched people come through the portal.

Kharon's voice changed as he spoke to the newcomers, as soon as the portal closed, preventing them from escaping. "Please stay in a single line. You will be sent to your final destination, depending on your crimes in life." Kharon waved an arm in the air and another portal appeared. This one was white. "This is what you humans would call judge and jury."

The people started to whisper. Some had frightened looks on their faces, other rolled their eyes, and the rest stood there shocked.

"Start walking!" Kharon barked.

The first person to walk up to the white portal was a teenage girl. She was covered in blood and most of her clothes was missing. She had a bullet wound on her head. She cried as she walked through the portal.

"Marcy Eldridge," Kharon spoke as the portal turned red, "You are sentence to eternity in Hell. Your crimes include the following: stealing, espionage, and murder."

Marcy gasped as she heard her sentence. "I only killed," she started in a Russian accent, "because those guys had raped me! They stole some thing from me that I will never get back! Is it wrong to get revenge on someone who ruined your life?"

Kharon was about to speak when Lucifer stepped upn shaking his head. "Killing is a sin, sweetheart. Even if someone ruined your life, getting revenge is not the way to go. Since you are the first person to walk through the portal, I want to welcome you to Hell." Lucifer held out his hand.

Shaking her head, Marcy slapped his hand away and yelled, "I am not staying here!" She took off running, trying to make it to the river. Don't know why. The river is toxic.

Lucifer sighed as raised his raised his left hand. Marcy floated in the air, absolutely confused. "You shouldn't have ran," Lucifer tsked as he snapped his fingers.

In an instant Marcy's neck made a snapping noise, which caused her to cry out in pain. Then she burst sinto flames. She screamed as the flames engulfed her.

The crowd gasps, horrified as they watched the girl scream, unable to move. As she pleaded for the torture to stop, her skin turned black. Then, her body disappeared, leaving the smell of burnt skin where she once floated.

"Now," Lucifer looked at the crowd, in his demon form, "Who's next?"

Remember to vote and share if you liked this chapter.

Seven Demaro Dellero

Once everyone was sorted, they were put on a boat that sent them to their final destination. Out of the thirty people that were sorted, only twelve were sent to heaven.

"What the Hell was that?' I yelled at Lucifer, once the last boat to heaven left.

"What do you mean?" Lucifer asked, staring at the boat until it disappeared from sight. Once it was gone, he turned and looked at me.

"Why did you torture that poor girl?"

"That girl was not poor, if anything she lived a life full of luxury and gold. She was the Russian's president's step-daughter."

"That's not what I meant!" I stomped my foot. "Why did you have to show off on her?"

"Because I am the King of the Underworld and I wanted to. Besides, it is my job to show no mercy on criminals."

"But what she did was not criminal, she killed a guy who ruined her life!" I cried.

"Hey!" Lucifer raised a hand, "I don't make the rules, I just enforce them. If you have a problem, I would suggest your talk to the guy who decided that killing was a sin. Besides, not only did she kill, but she stole and lie. Espionage, apparently, is a form of lying."

I was going to argue with him, but I decided against it. Instead, I glared at Lucifer and walked off. I know that he has a job to do, but why should a person be tortured until the end of time for doing what they were trained to do? How can a person so young be sentenced with an eternity of torture?

That made me think of Leven. How did he end up in this Hell? What did he do that was so horrific that sentenced him to this place?

I started to walk faster away from Lucifer. I was going to find out some answers.

"Raven?" Lucifer called, making me turn around. He was so far behind me. "Where are you going?"

"I am going to the house. I...I need some time away from you to think!" I yelled, taking off towards the house. "Don't even think about following me!" I did need time away from Lucifer but I wanted to find out what a person has to do to end up here.

"Has anyone seen Leven?" I asked around the house. I went from room to room, trying to find that boy. When you don't need him, he appears and when you want him, he's nowhere to be found. I was about to give up, and head back to my room when I found him. "Leven, darling! I was to speak to you," I approached the boy and pulled him into my room.

"Yes, Mistr-Miss Hunter?" Leven said as I motioned for him to sit on the bed. I had told him, after the first time he called me 'Mistress Hunter' to call me Miss Hunter. Mistress just sounded so...sexual.

I decided to get straight to the point. No use in beating around the bush on a sensitive subject. "I want you to tell me why you are in Hell."

"May I ask, what brought this on?" Leven asked.

"I saw something today that made me realize that the souls that are here may be here for stupid reasons," I answered. "Before you tell me why you are here, I want you to tell me how old were you when you died and how old are you now."

Leven frowned at me, shifting on the bed. I guess the subject is an uncomfortable one for him.

"Well, I was fifteen when I died. That was over three hundred and thirty-three years ago. I will tell you that my name wasn't always Leven. Before I died, my name was Seven. Now, I know that is a weird name to give a kid but growing up in the time I did, with the parents I had, I was predicted to commit the seven deadly sins before the age of eighteen. You have heard of the seven deadly sins, haven't you Miss?" Leven looked at me, embarrassment in his eyes.

"Yes, I have. They are Gula, Luxuria, Avaritia, Superbia, Tristitia, Ira, Vanagloria, and um...I forgot the last one," I said. Growing up alone, I had a lot of time on my hand to research stuff.

"It's Acedia. Now, during the time that I grew up in, most people were Christians. Well, my parents were not. They worshipped the Devil and they thought it a joke to name me Seven. My full name was Seven DeMarco Dellero. They would joke about how I would commit all the sins before I turned eighteen. With them as my influence and telling me that their way was the best way to live, I did what they predicted me to do. Only I committed the last of the sins by the time I turned fifteen."

I looked at him in a way that showed him that I didn't believe him. "You're honestly telling me that you did them all before you turned fifteen? That's a bit too much, don't you think?"

"It's the truth though, you can ask anyone, you can even ask him," Leven nodded towards the door.

"What the Hell are you doing here?" I asked Lucifer. "I told you to give me space!"

"I was going to give you space but I wanted to make sure that you arrived at the house safely, first. Besides, I decided that we have some matters to discuss."

"Well, I do not want to discuss them with you right now. I want to listen to Leven, so shush."

"Leven, tell her how you died," Lucifer smiled.

I looked at Leven, a bit curious. "Well, since my parents were devil worshippers, and he knew this, he visited them one night. It was the night before my sixteenth birthday. He showed up right in our living room, which scared almost scared the shit out of them. They were ecstatic to see him them and tried to please him, offering them all their money and anything else they could. But Lucifer did not want what they were offering. Oh no, he refused their gifts."

"Oh my God...they didn't," I whispered. I knew where this was going.

"Oh yeah, Miss. Lucifer wanted a sacrifice. He told them that if they sacrifice me, they would have a special little place in Hell. They told him that they would think about it. That night, thinking that they would never do such a thing, I went to sleep without giving the day a thought. The next thing I remember is waking up, tied to the front of the tree with my mom and dad with a knife in their hand. Their last words to me?" Leven laughed bitterly. "'Sorry, son, but we all knew this day would come. You were make for this purpose.' That was what my mom told me before she slit my throat."

"Oh my God!" I gasped, horrified. "I am so sorry."

Leven shrugged. "Not your fault Miss Hunter. They were devil worshippers and apparently God doesn't allow those type of people into heaven when they die...or when they commit suicide." When I looked at him confused, he continued. "Ever heard of Macbeth? Now remember the part where the wife commits suicide because she is overcome by grief and all that crap."

"Wait, so they killed themselves because they were upset that they killed you?" I asked.

Leven smiled, "Yeah, one could say that. That's what the papers said, anyways. But in reality, a thought was placed in their head to kill themselves by the one person who told them to sacrifice me." Leven laughed.

"That's horrible!" I said looking from Lucifer to Leven. They truly are horrible people. ----

Killing the Mother

I looked over at Lucifer to see him smiling. "You see, Angel, even I agree that sacrificing your children without asking them first is downright cruel. Besides, they were starting to get annoying. Ever heard of the Deadly Seven Sculptors? They were big in the late sixteen hundred's?" I shook my head 'no'. "Well, they were a couple who would kill people and pose them committing one of the seven deadly sins. They were never caught until I met up with them that night." Lucifer smiled at the memory. "Ah, what fun that was."

"So, where are they?" I asked.

"They're around here somewhere," he said. I noticed something that briefly flashed in his eyes. It was evil, and that scared me.

Shaking my head, I thanked Leven for taking the time to talk to me. Once Leven left the room, I turned to Lucifer. "What was so important that you needed to see me?"

Lucifer smiled and grabbed my hand. "Follow me."

"You're not going to take me to the top of a building again, are you?" I joked. The last time I followed Lucifer was to the top of the building where I almost died for like the fourth time.

"No, just follow me. You'll like it I promise." He smiled, which made me smile because it was a real genuine smile. He winked at me, which caused my heard to skip a beat.

Calm down, Raven. It was just a wink. Nothing more. I took deep breaths to calm my thoughts down.

Lucifer led me to a room that I have never seen before. "Where are we?" I asked when he unlocked the door.

Throwing the door open, he answered, "Welcome to the ballroom."

I smiled as I looked around the room. The ceiling was probably twenty feet high. There were twelve columns around the room. The room was painted a beautiful aquamarine color and the floors were a light grey with sparkles in them. "Is this granite under our feet?"

Lucifer smiled and nodded. "Yes, it is. Don't ask how much it cost because I won't tell you. Just know that when we have our ball, that'll introduce you to the demons and souls of the underworld, you will be the most ravishing creature down here."

I smiled at his comment. Should I be offended that he called me a creature?

"So, Mr. DeVil, what are we doing here?" I asked.

"Well, Miss Hunter, we are here to teach you to dance. I have decided that the ball will be in four days. That's four days we have to get you ball material ready."

"But, why do we need a ball? Why can't we just have like a Meet and Greet thing?"

Lucifer laughed, directing me out of the ballroom. "The last time I held a Meet and Greet was when Hell got a huge shipment of souls-over one thousand- sent here for a permanent living lifestyle. Let's just say that only about twelve of those souls didn't get fed on. So, yeah, if you want a Meet and Greet, I'd be more than happy to set it up. I can't guarantee that you won't be mistaken as a soul though."

"What the heck do you mean fed on?"

Lucifer gave me one of that ' are-you-flipping-stupid?' looks. "Even though demons don't really need to eat, they still enjoy the hunt. You know? They're down here for a reason and they-"

"How do you become a demon?" I asked.

"I'm glad that you are being serious about the whole thing."

"Well, since I am living down here, I guess I need to be prepared for anything that is thrown my way."

"True, true. This is going to blow your mind. A lot of demons are born. It all happens when male down here goes up to earth and they have sex with a human. The thing about being born a demon: the mother does not live through the childbirth. The demon child is normally inside the mother's womb for at least an entire year.

"There are not a lot of humans that know about the existence of Hell and demons. Now, I do not know why this happens exactly but when a demon child is inside the mother, he or sometimes she starts to starve the mother, taking all the nutrients that she takes in. The demon is basically killing the mother. Now, you have heard that when a woman is pregnant, she feels a strong desire to carry that baby to term, right?"

Horrified, I nodded. I knew where this was headed, but I couldn't bring myself to speak.

"Well, a woman carrying a demon child has an even stronger desire to carry that child. I think it has something to do with the child inside of her. They develop a brain after the first month and they can tell the mother what they are craving. It's a whole weird operation.

"Anyway, by the time that the child is ready to come into this world, the mother is practically dead. So, after the child is born, they eat the mother. I know that it may seem morbid, but it is actually a beautiful thing when I think about it. For the child, to eat the mother is like the final connection between the two. Think of it like this: the mother is already practically dead, so when the child comes out, her last purpose in life is to provide the baby with a good meal. If the baby doesn't eat the mother, it's like the child is rejecting the person who gave birth to it."

"Are you serious?!" I yelled. "You think that that is a beautiful thing? That's horrible!" I had to take a few minutes to calm down. That is- my mind could not handle that information. "So, are there any female demons?"

"Actually, most demons, like me, are males. Those who are female demons are very dangerous and very powerful. There are only a handful of female demons, a lot of them you will probably see at the ball. The thing about the females is they cannot get pregnant. Don't ask me why, because I honestly don't know. Any more questions?"

"No," I said, still trying to take in everything that he had just told me. So, does that mean that if I-if we- were to have a child together that I would die? That my child would slowly kill me over time? Shaking my head, I changed my train of thought. Raven, why the Hell are you thinking about that? You would have to get into bed with Lucifer and Lord knows that you are not ready for that. I mean yeah, he's a good-looking piece of meat that I wouldn't mind f-

"Raven, darling? Did you even hear a word I said? What do you think?" Lucifer stopped walking and looked at me.

"Huh? Yeah, sure. I would love to." I said, hoping I didn't agree to something I wouldn't normally agree to.

Lucifer's face brightens as he clasped his hands together. "Perfect! We're going to teach you how to use your abilities."

"Wait what?! How are you going to do that?"

"Let's just say that it involves fighting my most talented soldier." Lucifer smiled and laughed.

Oh, please don't let me die, I silently prayed.

The Kiss

"Where are we going?" I asked as Lucifer pulled me through the seventh room. We stopped right in front of a pair of double doors.

"Boy, am I glad that I do not have to listen to you ask that question on more time," Lucifer said as he opened the doors to the room. "Raven, this is the old ball room. We use this room for public gatherings now. "

I gasped in amazement as I stepped into the room. It was beautiful! The ceiling, I estimated, was about twenty feet from the ground. The room had six white pillars around the room, which seemed to make the room even more fancy. At the front of the room held sort of a stage where two thrones were stationed. The room had silver, royal purple, and black curtains up all around the room. The room was tiled with granite, which really had a sparkle to it. The room could have probably fit my entire town in it.

"It's amazing!" I looked at Lucifer and smiled.

"Thanks," Lucifer smiled as he grabbed my hand and led me through the room. "This is where we used to hold the balls. Now that I think if it. We can have the ball in this room: it's bigger than the newer ball room, I showed you earlier. This is where we will introduce you to the souls, servants, the most powerful demons and then some. The world will know that you are mine."

I pulled away from him and stared at him. "What makes you say I am yours?"

"I just assumed that since you decided to live down here with me that you chose me," Lucifer said quietly.

I actually haven't given the whole thing a second thought as soon as I was brought down here. Everything just happened so quickly that I didn't really question anything after it happened.

"Raven Hunter who do you choose?" A voice, that turned out to be God's voice, asked.

"I choose-" I started as the ground came awfully close. "I choose," I couldn't believe my entire life had led up to this one moment. "I choose both. I choose them both!" I cried. I threw my hands out in front of my face, as if they would protect me from dying.

"So, it shall be," God answered, and I felt him leave my mind.

In that moment, a sharp pain exploded from my back and I screamed. I had never felt anything like it before.

"Fly!" I heard Micheal and Lucifer yell at the same time. They had both jumped off the building after me and was about a yard behind me.

"What?" I yelled back, confused.

"Just think fly!" Micheal yelled.

Fly? I thought to myself, still confused.

In that moment, just before I hit the ground, I was violently jerked upwards. I had stopped falling and I seemed to hover over about five feet from the ground.

"Raven! You're flying!" Micheal said.

"What?" I asked as I looked up. I reached behind me and felt feathers. I looked behind me and I saw two wings: one black and one white. "What the heck?!" I screamed, scared.

In that moment, my wings retracted, and I fell to the ground.

"What did you choose?" Lucifer whispered, a horrified look on his face, as soon as they touched ground.

"I chose you both," I said as I stood up. "What happened to my wings?"

"That's amazing!" Micheal cried as he picked me up and spun me around. "As for your wings, they have a mind of their own. They come when called and disappear when you are scared. They are weird."

"So, what happens now?" I inquired.

"You have to decide where you want to spend the rest of your life," Lucifer sadly said.

"Why are you sad?" I asked Lucifer, walking up to him.

Micheal answered for Lucifer, "He thinks that given the choice, you are going to come and live with me."

"Well," I started, "you're not wrong."

"Raven, before you go with Micheal can I give you a kiss?" Lucifer asked.

"What? Why?" I was confused. Why would he want a kiss?

"I just want to see something," he said.

I looked over at Micheal who nodded. Shrugging, I stepped closer to Lucifer. "Do not try anything. I will not hesitate to start kicking," I warned.

"I'll miss that fire," Lucifer said as he leaned closer to me.

Taking a deep breath, I closed my eyes. This was going to be my first kiss ever. My first kiss will be with the devil. What if he takes my soul? What if he kills me? What if-

In that moment, I felt his lips on mine. I jumped a bit when he grabbed my waist and pulled me closer. It was weird. I started to feel warm. My entire body seemed to heat up as he kissed me.

It was weird because in that moment I felt safer with him than I have ever felt with Micheal. "We need to go, Raven," Micheal spoke. Even though I knew he was right next to me, he sounded so far away.

Suddenly, I felt an electrical surge course through my body. I gasped and pulled away. The moment I looked into Lucifer's eyes, I saw my entire future with him. Not literally but I knew he was the only one who would truly protect.

"Raven, we need to go," Micheal said, grabbing my hand.

"No," I pulled away from him. "I changed my mind. I want to stay with Lucifer."

I looked at Lucifer who had a slight smile on his face. "Face it bro, even though she chose us both, you still lost."

"Let's go, Raven. We're going home." Lucifer held out his hand, and I took it. We walked away from Micheal. Lucifer waved his hand a portal appeared.

"Raven!" Micheal yelled. "If you walk through that portal, I will no longer be able to protect you."

"When have you truly protected me?" I yelled back. "Lucifer was always there for me. Micheal, I love you but I am destined to be with Lucifer. Besides, we have no future together and we never will."

Micheal was speechless as I stared at him. "Just go," he said. "Just go and enjoy your life in Hell."

That was the last time I saw Micheal. That was two days ago.

"Raven, are you okay?" Lucifer asked wiping away a tear.

"Yeah, let's go," I said, walking ahead of a worried Lucifer.

"Raven, I have agreed to educated you on a thing or two before you can fight. If you have any questions, please ask." Miss Lillie smiled at me.

"Okay, fine, educate away."

"Each angel, even Lucifer have abilities. There are some angels who can grant wishes, if you will, some who can plant suggestions in other's mind. There are a lot of abilities that angels have. The one downside of an ability is that angels only have one ability. So, when it comes to fighting or train- ing, they can't do anything beyond the ability they have. That is, unless you are Lucifer."

"What about me?" I asked. "What ability will I have?"

"I don't know. No one ever knows until the time comes. Most angels know their ability by the time they reach puberty. With you Raven, it may be different. Even though you are an angel, you are the first of your kind. Every angel known, excluding you, is either half angel or a person God has blessed into an Angel. You are the first full bred angel, if you will. So, you may have one ability or you may get a multitude of abilities."

"What is one ability that is super rare?" I asked.

"I'll answer this question then I have to go. The ability to slow down time. Only one person in the entire world holds that ability." Miss Lillie stood up.

"Really, who?" I questioned.

"Micheal," Miss Lillie answered.

My face paled at the mention of his name, but I ignored it. "What did he use his ability for?"

"To save the love of his life," Miss Lillie replied. She walked to the door and opened it.

"Wait!" I yelled after her, "Did he save her?"

"Him," Miss Lillie corrected.

"Did he save him?" I corrected myself.

"No, he didn't. His lover died in his arms and he has never loved another person again," Miss Lillie responded before she shut the door behind her.

Fighting Zaphara

"Raven, this is who you are going to be fighting." Lucifer pointed to Zaphara. "She is one of my most skilled fighters," Lucifer complimented.

"Dude, I am your only skilled fighter, and you know it." Zaphara punched Lucifer in the shoulder.

"That is true. Now, Raven, this training exercise is only to help you find or use the abilities that you have stored in your genetic coding." Lucifer looked over to Zaphara. "Do not hurt her. Okay? I need her in one piece."

"Yeah, whatever brother. I won't hurt her...much." Zaphara looked over at me and winked. "Besides, I'll stay away from her pretty little face as much as possible, deal?"

"Zaphara," Lucifer warned. "You will not hurt her. If you feel the urge to, please do what we talked about. Okay?"

"What do you mean, if she feels the urge to?" I asked. I am not going to fight a girl who has been trained by Lucifer if she cannot control herself.

"Zaphara is half demon, Raven. This means that once in a while, especially with her, her demon likes to show up in a place of battle. However, since this is not a real battle, her demon should be sleeping. You should be good, though. I have seen you fight and you're not threatening enough to wake her demon."

I was about to defend myself when Zaphara interrupted. "Brother, can we please get this over with?" Zaphara asked. "I actually have a date tonight and I would like to not be late."

"Fine," Lucifer snapped. "Raven, darling, if you need me, I will be up there, behind that glass, okay?" Lucifer pointed up the wall, where sure enough was a glass separating the two rooms.

"Okay," I said. As soon as I said nodded, left the room and went to the showroom.

He pressed a button that allowed us to hear him. "Okay, children. I want a nice clean fight. No cheating. Are you ready?" He looked over to me and I nodded. He looked over to Zaphara who nodded too. "Ready, set, fight!" he yelled.

I got into a fighting position and Zaphara smiled at me. "You ready Kitten?"

"Ready as I'll ever be," I mumbled.

Zaphara smiled, this time showing pointy teeth, and I gulped. Oh Lord. Did she have those when she came in?

I decided to make the first move as I charge towards her. My fist drove forward, which only hits air, as Zaphara ducks out of the way, she then reciprocated with a few blows of her own. Her fist collides with my right, the force behind it causing pain to flare, I stumble back; hissing between my teeth.

"Come on!" Lucifer yelled. "Give me a good cat fight!"

Zaphara and I looked up at Lucifer. I glance over at Zaphara who gave him the finger, I took that opportunity to strike.

I kick Zaphara in the stomach as hard as I could and she doubles over, clutching her stomach, standing over her, I then bring my elbow down into her back and down to the floor she went. "Yes!" I smiled as I look up at Lucifer. "That wasn't so-"

I didn't get to finish that sentence as a fist came flying and plows into my face. I felt and heard something crack and I cradle my nose. "Shit!" I yelled. "I think you broke my nose." At that moment, blood starts to trickle from my nose. "Fuck! You did!"

Zaphara's lips curl up into an evil smile, as I take a step forward, wiping my nose with the back of my hand, which wasn't bleeding as badly as before. I inhale deeply and close my eyes, my heart was beating erratically in my chest. Come on, Raven, you got this. Just calm down. Just breathe. My heart started to slow in pace, until going back to its normal speed.

I opened my eyes and all sounds around me became a dull flutter of noise. Just in time, I see Zaphara thrust her fist outward toward me. Taking a step to the side, I dodged her punch, watching as her hand drives past my face at the speed of a snail. It was like she was moving in slow motion. Is she? It was like a dream. The room around me was like a hazy focus of a camera. My focus just on the both of us, everything else was blurred.

Zaphara threw a series punches, trying to hit me wherever she could but I dodged each of them, easily. She threw another punch, aiming for my face. I quickly grab her hand, spinning her around and twisting her arm behind her back, kicking the back of her leg. Her knees gave out beneath her and she falls.

The trance that I seemed to be in, broke when Zaphara sharply cried out.

I watched as she slowly stood up, making me back away. Zaphara glared viciously at me, her eyes bleeding into black. She sneered at me, her face taking on murdous feature. I took one step towards her, observing her expression and posture for any signs of attacks. She brought her hands up in front of her and then snapped them down; palms spread out as two chains flew out from her wrist. At the end of the chains were what I like to call devil daggers.

"Zaphara!" Lucifer yelled, catching my attention to him. He ran over to the door and Zaphara nodded her head, and I guessed locked the door to the room, so Lucifer could not escape. "No! Fight it!"

I gaze up where Lucifer was and shouted; "What is going on?"

"Raven, Zaphara has locked me from leaving the room. I can't teleport out of here because of certain reasons. You are going to have to get her to calm down. That is your only option!"

"How do I-" Zaphara, at that moment swings her chains at me, and I ducked, dropping to my hands.

"I will make you pay!" Zaphara roared, swinging one of her chains at me, one dagger slashing my forearm.

I wince, grabbing hold of the new wound and look back at her. "Zaphara, please calm down," I say, holding a hand out in front of me to show her I meant no harm.

She didn't get the memo. Her chains kept coming after me, twirling them over her head like a lasso, and then released them until they came flying towards me. I darted out of the away, the sound of the knife's scraping against the spot I once stood in. Quickly, she reels in her chains and send them back at me at the speed of light, the daggers slicing my arms and neck up.

"Stop!" I cry as I run across the room, dodging her chains. I rush over to the door, hoping to make it out of the room alive. The moment I put my hand on the handle, I heard the lock click. "No!" I yelled, as I tried to open the door. "Help!" I screamed as I pounded on the door. "Someone help me!"

"No one is going to help a pathetic Angel in Hell, kitten. You're nothing but a snack to them," Zaphara whispers in my ear, which caused me to gasp.

She grabs a fist full of my hair and drug me to the middle of the room, with my feet flailing. "Oh, Luci! Lucifer!" she taunted, throwing me on my side. "I want you to watch as your most skilled fighter snaps your precious little angel's neck!"

"Zaphara! Stop!" Lucifer snarls.

Zaphara cackles as she grasps one of her death chains and wrapped it around my neck, choking me.

I fought as hard as I could, struggling to release myself, her grip tightening around the chain, which the same reaction around my neck. Lucifer pleaded for Zaphara to calm down, stop, and open the door.

Zaphara leaned down, her breath blowing against my ear, "That's right, little kitten. Go to sleep. You never were good enough for my brother." Black dots begin to crawl from the edge of my eyes, my vision blurring in and out, I stop fighting. I let my hands drop to the ground, limp. My right hand falls on something along the floor, side-glance at the object and I see it to be the end of Zaphara's chain.

With the last of my strength, I curl my fingers around the dagger, my grip tightening and I plunge the weapon deeply into Zaphara's leg, blood immediately beginning to pool around the tip. She screams and lets go of her chains along with me. I scramble away, crawling then stumbling to my feet making it to the other side of the room.

Zaphara shierks, "You are going to pay for that, you bitch!"

I could hear Lucifer yelling out for the guards. A blur of movements, and Zaphara zips in front of me, breathing heavily. "Say your prayers, kitten." she brings her chains up behind her, springing herself into the air, letting out a warrior cry, releasing her hold on the chain.

I threw my hands in front of my face, in hopes I could protect myself.

"No!" Lucifer and I yelled as Zaphara brought the chains down on me, everything slowing down as they grew closer by the minute.

She's Dead

"Raven, wake up!" Lucifer screamed in my ear.

I sat up in a panic. What happened? Everything around me was darker than usual, mostly dark grey and black. "Shit!" I yell. I was shadow walking mode.

I stand up and observe my surrounding. There were a bunch of people around me. In the far right of the room, stood Zaphara and Miss Lillie. Zaphara had her head on Miss Lillie's shoulder, crying. Why was she crying? I asked myself.

Leven stood next to Lucifer who was next to my body, on the ground. Caleb and Antony were a few steps behind them.

"Miss Lillie!" I waved my hand in the air. "Miss Lillie!" I called again, when she didn't look my way. I knew that she was the only who could see me when I was in this realm. But am I really in the shadow realm? I wondered. This realm is so much darker and colder than the regular one.

I tried to walk over to Miss Lillie but found that I couldn't go but five steps away from my body no matter how hard I tried. I looked back at my sleeping body, and saw what looked like a white rope going from my body to around my foot.

"What is going on?!" I yelled, when I couldn't break the rope. At that moment, I felt a sudden pain shoot through my body and I doubled over. I was hit with another wave of pain, and this time I fell to the ground. I could barely breathe. It felt like someone was slowly chocking me.

Lucifer bent down over my body and held his ear over my mouth. "She is still not breathing!" Lucifer yelled, sitting back up. "Somebody do something!"

"Lucifer, she's dead. We can't do anything else," Caleb said. "None of us in this room have what is needed to bring her back."

I'm dead? Bring me back? I thought to myself. What does he mean? I'm not dead. I can still see them all, I shook my head. But, Raven, that would explain why everything is so different, so cold. You actually are- I cried out as the pain got stronger. "No!" I yelled. "I am not dead. I refuse to believe I am dead. I haven't even lived my life yet."

"I refuse to believe that she is dead!" Lucifer yelled, his voice breaking. "I did not wait over a million years for my soul mate just to have her die three days after she accepted my world! She has many more years ahead of her. So, someone better figure out how to fix this or I swear to His High and Mighty I will make sure that for the rest of your undead lives, I will feel the worse possible pain you have ever felt!" Lucifer roared, and the room shook.

"She's not dead," Miss Lillie spoke up, walking to the center of the room. "She's in the Between."

"What is that?" Caleb asked.

"That's where she is not dead but not alive. Look at is like this: You all see a so-called-dead body, right there," Miss Lillie pointed to my body. "But I can tell you that she's still alive, in a way. She's tethered to her body."

"How do we bring her back?" Lucifer questioned.

"We need someone who has been to the Between and back. There's only one person who has ever done that," Zaphara said, joining the crowd.

Lucifer glared at Zaphara and motioned for her to continue.

Zaphara opened her mouth to answer but Leven beat her to it. "Mazel."

"No." Caleb shook his head. "We can't let Mazel near her. She'll for sure kill-"

Lucifer held up his hand, which stopped Caleb from talking. "Antony, go get Mazel."

Antony bowed his head, and took off. For a big guy, he could run. A few minutes later, he appeared with Mazel by his side.

"What do you want, Luci," Mazel growled. "I was about to get some fine piece of meat in me when your buffoon of a bodyguard interrupted us."

"Mazel!" Lucifer frantically beckoned her over to my body. "Please, please help her."

"Woah!" Mazel smirked walking over to my body, "Who finally took out the Princess?"

"Mazel, please. Just save her. I need you bring her back from the Between," Lucifer begged.

The pain started up again, and this time, I screamed out. I laid on the floor, in a fetal position.

"What is in it for me?" Mazel asked, folding her arms. "I don't even like the bitch."

"Anything!" Lucifer screamed, "As long as you can bring her back. Please!" He held his hand out, offering it to her.

"Why?" Mazel asked again. "Why do you want me to do this?"

"Because." Lucifer said, as if it was the answer to her question.

"Because why?" Mazel pressed.

"Because...because I fucking love her!" Lucifer screamed. "I love her, dammit! I love her more than I have ever loved anybody. She is my soul mate and I am hers, and if you cannot bring her back, I will literally die. So, for once in your life, do something good and save her."

The look on Mazel's face melted away. After a moment of standing there, staring at him, she took his hand and sat down next to my body. "I'll see what I can do."

She pulled my buttoned shirt apart, revealing my bra. Lucifer started to protest but she held up her hand. "I need access to bare skin or I will torch her clothes," she explained. Lucifer nodded and motioned for her to continue.

Taking a deep breath, she pressed her hands together, and whispered something. Pulled her hands apart and touched my chest.

I watched, from the ground, as my body jerked upwards.

"Again!" Lucifer yelled.

A new pain in my chest, appeared. I grimaced as I propped myself up with my left arm.

Mazel pressed her hands against my chest, again and my body jerked. The pain grew stronger. "Luci, she's dead."

"Again!" Lucifer yelled, shaking his head.

"Luci," Mazel whispered, "How long has she been in the Between? I probably can't bring her back."

"Just do it again!" Lucifer pleaded.

Sighing, Mazel shook her head. "If this doesn't work this time, you are going to have to accept the fact that she is gone."

"Do it!" Lucifer yelled. "Give it all you have!"

Mazel nodded and closed her eyes. Rolling her head back, she threw her hands in the air, and a blue electrical current sparked between her two hands. She then brought her hands closer together, like she was holding a ball. She looked at my body and brought it down on my chest.

Lucifer's ragged breathing was the last thing I remember as my arm gave out, and my head hit the ground.

"Raven. Raven, honey, wake up," Lucifer whispered.

I opened my eyes and saw Lucifer's face close to mine. He was playing with my hair.

"What happened? I asked, jerking away from him. "The last thing I remember is Zaphara's chains." I sat up. I was in bed, in a different set of clothing than before. Panic started to form in my chest. "What did you do?"

"Relax, Angel. You're still pure. I had the maid change your clothes to nightwear."

I slowly nodded as relief flooded me. I believe him. "So, what happened?"

"Well, let's just say that I will never underestimate you again. You are strong enough to wake up Zaphara's demon. Right before Zaphara brought her chains down on you, your wings unfolded from your back, and protected you. When her chains connected with your wings, there was a big spark of blue, that formed around your wings, which I think was sort of like our energy balls we make. The spark sent Zaphara across the room, and you collapsed.

'As soon as I entered the room, I rushed over to you. I grabbed you just before your head hit the ground. 'Save me," you whispered in my ear, before you passed out."

"How long was I dead?"

"You were not dead. You were in a place called the between for seven minutes. It's a miracle you're alive. Mazel brought you back."

"She did?" I asked. "That is right," I mumbled, "She did. I remember."

"You remember what?" Lucifer asked, grabbing my shoulders.

"I remember. Leven said that she was the only one who had the capability to bring me back. I remember you crying over my body. I remember you...I remember you confessing that you love me," I gasped, holding my hand over my mouth.

'Yeah," Lucifer shrugged. "So, what?"

"Tell me you were joking."

I watched as Lucifer fell silent. He doesn't actually love me, right?

Meet My Wife

I stared at Lucifer, hoping for one specific answer. If he loves me then I will be the-

"No," Lucifer replied, flatly. He walked went to the closet and opened the door.

"What?" I whisper. Maybe I didn't hear him right?

Lucifer shook his head and sighed. He walked into the closet and mumbled something, that I couldn't quite hear. A minute later, he walked back out of the closet, buttoning up the shirt he put on.

"What did you say?" I ask him.

Sighing, dramatically, Lucifer walked over to the bed, still buttoning up his shirt. "Raven, honey, listen. I am the King of the Underworld, the Ruler of Hell, the rightful owner of everything that is evil. You, on the other hand, are...how shall I say it? You're a delicate flower. When you sneeze, nothing happens. When I sneeze, the whole underworld shakes. You get me?"

"No."

"Raven. We are two different people. I am pure evil. You are...what ever you are. We are totally opposites."

"I don't understand? Is that your way of telling me opposites attract and that you love me or that-" I started to say.

"No!" Lucifer yelled. "I don't love you! I only told Mazel that I loved you in order to keep you alive. Mazel is the type of person who believes in love. She'll do anything for love. Pathetic really. Love can't exist down here, only pain and suffering and screams."

"But-" Tears started to form in my eyes.

"Get it through your skull! I don't love you! Why would I love you? Raven, I need a strong, and capable fighter. I need someone who can fight her own battles and not faint at the sight of blood. I need someone who can match my level of craziness and be okay with who I am. Do you understand?"

Taking a deep breath, I nodded. "I understand," I told him. "I was hoping you would say no."

Something in Lucifer's eyes, changed but I couldn't tell what.

"If you are done being an ass, I think I am going to go." I stood up from the bed and walked to the door, opening it.

"Where are you going?" Lucifer asked.

"Where I am going is none of your damn business," I spat. "You're not my boyfriend so why would you care."

"But-" Lucifer started to say something, but I cut him off, not wanting to hear it.

"Just leave me the Hell alone. If you think I need you, you're wrong," I said before I slammed the bedroom door.

He's an asshole Raven. You definitely do not need him. What you need is to learn how to fight properly and stand on your own two feet.

After I left the bedroom, I decided to explore the house a bit. Even though I knew what almost every room was, I still wanted to explore. Anything to get away from Lucifer. That was almost two hours ago.

I was about to go back to the bedroom, when I decided to go to Lucifer's study room. I knew that it would be locked, so I checked behind the picture of Medusa and pulled a key out. I may or may not have made an extra copy of Lucifer's key and hid it.

I unlocked the room, and shivered. It was so cold in here. He liked to keep it cold because of the portal that was in the room. The portal could only function at a certain temperature, but it wasn't activated at the moment.

I decided to look around the room. It was what you would expect from a boring office room. Two walls were lined with books, from floor to ceiling and a bunch of maps, and sticky notes lined the other walls. The room was a mess!

I walked over to the book shelf and decided to pick out a book to read. The first book I picked, I couldn't read it. It was in some kind of ancient writing. The second book was the same.

Sighing, I reached for a book called, The Guide to Torture. I tried to pull if off the shelf, but it wouldn't budge. Growling, I tipped the top of the book towards me and the weirdest thing happened: the other wall that was lined with books, folded into the wall, revealing another hallway.

"Fuck you," I cursed at the book as I made my way to the secret hallway. "Now, why would you not tell me about this?" I asked.

I walked to the end of the hallway, where I was greeted by a door. "Please be unlocked," I whisper, as I turn the knob. It was.

Smiling, I opened the door and found some stairs that seem to lead to a basement.

Raven, maybe you shouldn't go down there. Haven't you seen the movies? This is how people die.

"Oh, hush up," I said aloud, to the voice in my head as I descended down the steps. "I'll be careful, I promise."

When I got the bottom of the stairs, I heard voices.

Being as quiet as I could, I walked to investigate. I stopped right in front of a dark purple door, that was opened a crack.

"Oh, baby," a female voice behind the door said. "You like that don't you?"

"Yes," another voice whimpered. It was also a girl.

"What he did to you want not fair. It is his fault. God, he did a number on you." The person sighed. "Just scoot a little closer. Lay on your stomach. Let me help you forget all about your pain."

I heard some moving around, and covers rustling. I stepped closer to the door, trying to listen. I could hear some other noises, but couldn't identify what they were.

"How does that feel?" Asked the first person.

"It hurts," the second person replied.

"How about now?"

"It still hurts." The person was silent for a few seconds. The person raised their voice, "Stop. You're hurting me."

I was about to go back where I came from when I heard a muffled scream. Reacting, I threw the door open, ready to attack. I stopped short when I saw what was going on.

Miss Lillie was half naked and sitting on someone, who seemed to be completely naked except for underwear on.

I stood there, with my mouth wide open.

"Oh my God." Miss Lillie jumped off of the person, so fast that she tripped on her own feet.

"How did you get down here?" Miss Lillie asked once she put a shirt back on. "Nobody but a few people are supposed to know how to get down here."

"I um...I wanted to read and a torture book and...what the hell did I just witness. Why did she scream? Why are you both practically naked?"

"I was nursing her wounds, Raven. Lucifer did a number on her."

I was about to ask who it was, when the person raised their head and looked at me.

"Hey, Raven," Zaphara whispered.

"What happened to you?" I asked. She had a black eye and a busted lip.

"Nothing much," she tartly replied. "Lucifer just thought I needed to be punished."

"Well, that does not look that ba-" I stopped talking when Zaphara sat straight up.

Her body was covered in nasty bruises and cuts.

"Um, Zap? You may want to cover yourself. Your nipples are exposed," Miss Lillie said, handing Zaphara a shirt.

"Why did he do that?" I asked, whispering. What the hell happened to her?

"Let's just say that after Mazel brought your back, Lucifer decided to have a 'little talk with me'. Apparently almost killing you was a bad thing."

"But you're Lucifer's sister why would he....wait...why are you two down here in this room together half naked?"

"Raven, look around, this is my room," Miss Lillie told me. "This is where I reside when I am not on Earth. As for why we are in this room together: Raven, meet Zaphara Liizel, my wife."

No Soul

"**Y**our wife?" I repeated. Did I hear her right? She's a...what?

Miss Lillie smiled. "Yes, Raven, I am what you children call today, a lesbian. We have been married for one hundred and fifteen years. We dated about fifty years before we got married."

"Holy shit," I whispered. "That's a lot of years. So, are you two a secret or...?" I trailed off and held my hand up. I thought I heard someone crying, but as I tried to listen for the noise again, it stopped.

"Nah, almost everyone down here knows about us. You'll hear Lucifer tell you how love cannot survive down here. That is not true. We both love each other and will always love each other as long as we live."

"That's so sweet. I-" I stopped talking because I heard crying. "Okay. Tell me that you all hear that."

Miss Lillie looked at Zaphara, who looked at me. "Nope," they both said at the same time.

"Okay. You were say-" The crying started up again and this time, I couldn't ignore it. "Um, I'm going to go. I will uh talk to you all later."

I walked out of the room, and down the hallway. As I approached the last door on the right, I heard talking. I recognized the voice to be Mazel's.

"To live in a world where love can't exist is worse than living in the Between."

I slowly pushed the door open, which, thankfully, didn't creak as I stepped into the room. Mazel's cries seemed to have stopped right as soon as I entered the room because all she was doing now was sniffling, her back was facing me.

I shivered as cold air escaped from its prison, wrapping around me. The room that Mazel was in, was built in stone from top to bottom. In the center of the room was an altar, which Mazel stood in front of it. She wasn't directly in front of it because I could see the altar. On top of the altar was a metal cage that held, what looked like, a dagger in it. Chains wrapped around the cage, but one lock held the chains together, in place.

I slowly started walking towards Mazel, careful not to make a sound. She reached into her pocket and pulled out a key. I watched her as she inserted the key into the lock and the chains all fell to the ground.

Sighing, Mazel opened the cage and pulled out the dagger.

"You want to know what the worse part about living here is?" Mazel asked, turning to me, throwing the key at me, which I managed to catch.

"How did you-?" I looked at the key for a second and put it in my pocket.

"The fact that love, the purest emotion known to all kind, can't exist in a place as tainted and horrendous as Hell," Mazel said, as she walked closer to me, dagger in hand.

"You see, I thought everything was perfect between Lucifer and me before you came along. Do you know how many long nights we spent together in that bed you two, now share?" she asked.

I shook my head, not wanting to say anything to the upset demon with a dagger in her hand.

"Three hundred and sixty-five years!" she screamed, tears running down her face. "I loved each and every moment of it too. You know, they say that demons don't souls, right? That when they die forever, forgotten?" Mazel laughed, twirling the dagger in her hand. "I became a demon almost a thousand years ago. Before I died and became a slave to Lucifer, I did bad deeds for people in exchange for sex. I guess, I thought, eventually I would find my true love. I was wrong."

Mazel gripped the dagger by the blade so tight that blood slowly started to drip on the floor. Mazel hissed and dropped the dagger. With lightning speed, she grabbed the dagger before it hit the floor. My mouth dropped open as she continued talking.

"Do you know how hard it is for someone like me to live a life of loneliness? Being with Lucifer, in that bed, was the only thing that made me feel like I was loved. But I guess it is true, demons can't love if they don't have a heart, a soul."

"What are you talking about?" I asked, taking a step back, away from her.

"Oh, Lucifer didn't tell you?" Mazel looked at me for a minute, searching for something, I guess before she burst out laughing. "Oh, my! He didn't tell you. No matter how much he professes his love to you, he can't mentally love you. He has no soul to love you with. I don't know why I saved you. I knew he couldn't love you. He just believes that if he can keep you alive, he holds the most powerful tool in the world. You know that, right? You're nothing but a tool to him. You're the first of your kind."

"That is not-"

"True? Ha! It is. When I saved you, brought you back from the Between, I asked to collect on my bargain. I wanted him to love me or at least spend one more day in bed with me. He refused. He has never refused me!" she screamed.

"I thought if I gave myself to Lucifer, I would live the life I always wanted. Boy, was I wrong. I am nothing but a bed toy to him. I'm done, though. I'm tired of being nothing but someone he can bed.

"This dagger is the only way to stop this pain that I feel. I know it isn't possible for me to feel any kind of emotion, but I do. So, why don't you leave me be so I can rid the one thing that is causing me to hurt?

"I won't let you kill Luci-" I started but stopped when I saw Mazel grip the dagger with both hands and raise it above her head.

I charged towards her and before she could bring it down on herself. I kicked her in the stomach, which caused her to cry out and drop the dagger. While she was gathering her breath, I grabbed the dagger and threw it into the cage and quickly locked the cage back up.

"No! I am not going to let that happen. Think of how Lucifer would feel if you were no longer here for him?"

"He doesn't care!" Mazel screamed, collapsing to the floor, crying. "He doesn't care," she said a little more quietly. "When I told him that I couldn't live without his love, you know what he told me? 'Then don't. Mazel, in this world, I can't afford to love someone. You know I can't and I know you can't. So, why don't you do us a favor and either kill yourself or go back to your room?'"

I gasped. "Lucifer would not have told you that."

"Oh yeah?" Mazel said in a challenging voice. "Do you even know why that dagger was locked up, hidden, in a secret room? That dagger is the only thing that can truly kill an immortal. It is said that God made it in case he had to kill Lucifer. Lucifer stole the dagger and kept it locked up here." She shook her head.

"So?" I said. "That doesn't prove-"

"When Lucifer told me either kill myself or go back to my room, he held out the key that opens that little box. Do you still believe that Lucifer cares about me?"

Kidnapped

"You're wrong about love not existing here." I told Mazel after a few minutes of staring at her. "Zaphara and Miss Lillie love each other."

"You are so stupid," Mazel said, standing up. "Those two are not really demons. Zaphara is half demon and half human, so she is one of the lucky few that still managed to hold on to half of her soul. Lillian? She's not even a demon. She's...I don't even know what the term for her is."

"But-"

"You know what? I do not have time for this." Mazel walked out the door, and I followed her. "I have to dress this wound. That cut hurts like a bitch." She showed me her hand, which was still bleeding but the wound was turning purple.

"Is that normal?" I asked as we walked past Miss Lillie's bedroom. Mazel was about twelve steps ahead of me. She opened another door, which led to another set of stairs.

She was at the top of the stairs. "The dagger is like holy water for vampires. One cut can seriously damage a demon." She pushed in a stone to the wall, which opened up the bookshelf. "That is why I need to get back to my room before-"

The wall shut behind her before I reached the top of the step. "Mazel!" I yelled as I tried to open up the wall that was between us. "Mazel!"

I frantically tried to find the stone that opened up the wall. On the other side of the wall, I heard yelling and what seemed like fighting. Then, it ended with a thud.

I finally found the stone and pressed it into the wall. The wall opened, and I stepped into the main entrance of the house. I opened the door to Lucifer's study, and I screamed when I saw Mazel on the ground, a huge gash on her side, a pool of blood around her.

"Oh my God!" I ran over to her, and dropped to my knees, putting my hand over her wound. "Mazel are you-"

She grabbed a fistful of my hair and yanked my head down to the ground. "Bitch, run," she hoarsely said, through gritted teeth.

"What? No! I'm not leaving you behind," I said, as I take my hands off her wound and try to pry her hands away from my hair.

"Raven, you need to-" Mazel's eyes, suddenly got wide as she whispered, "Watch out."

I turned around just in time to see a guy, I've never seen before, pull out a Katondra and press it to my stomach.

I cried out in pain, as he slid the button on the side down, that activated the taser thing. The pain spread throughout my body, which caused it to feel like it was on fire. "Stop, please," I pleaded.

"That's enough," another voice, I have heard before, barked. "Just knock her out."

"Yes, Master Caleb," the guy said, as he pulled the Katondra away from me and hit me in the head with the butt of the weapon.

"Raven. Hey, Raven, wake up," a voice in the room, whispered.

"Huh?" I mumbled. "Go away."

"Raven, please. You have to open your eyes. We've been kidnapped."

Sighing, I groaned as I opened my eyes. "Where are we?" I asked as I saw Mazel, sitting across from me, chained to the wall. I could move my arms a bit, but they were chained too. I had a lot more slack to move them, than Mazel, though.

"Why are we chained?" I asked. "What happened?" I looked around the room, trying to find any clues that could tell me where we were.

We were in a room, that I guess, was part of a dungeon. Three out of four walls were solid while the fourth wall had bars.

"Mazel, where are your clothes?" I asked her. I can't believe it wasn't the first thing I noticed. Mazel had some sort of cloth wrapped around her breasts and underwear on. Her wound was stitched up pretty good.

"I don't know. I woke up like this. I guess they had to strip me in order to dress my wound. Wouldn't be the first time I woke up with practically no clothes one. But never mind that. Raven, who was that guy that was that older guy that was standing by that little kid when I came in-" Mazel stopped talking and shook her head. "Never mind. You were uncon-"

"Caleb," I whispered horrified, as I remembered the name my attacker said. "No. It couldn't have been."

"Yeah. That's his name." Mazel growled. "That's who attacked me. If I see his ass again, I'm going to rip his throat out and-"

"And do what honey?" Caleb asked as he opened up the bar to the cell. "What exactly are you going to do? You're in chains, remember? I can do whatever I want to you and you can't do shit. You know why? Because those chains are indestructible against demons." He walked up to Mazel and smiled. "So, if I wanted to do this-" He kicked Mazel where her stitches were, multiple times. "You wouldn't be able to do anything about it."

"Stop it!" I yelled as Mazel cried out. "You're hurting her."

Caleb stopped and looked at me. "Darling, you cannot seriously tell me that you care about her? She tried to kill you the first time you two saw each other!"

"She's not a bad person once you get to know her," I told him. "She is just misunderstood."

"That's where you're wrong, doll. Anyway, I came here to give you food. It's been more than twelve hours since you last ate."

Caleb snapped his fingers and the guy who attacked me earlier brought in a tray of food. "I'll be back soon and we can talk about your purpose here."

Caleb left the room, with the guy trailing behind him.

Sighing, I looked at the food on the tray. I was hungry. On the tray, were a sandwich and some kind of soup. I reached for the food as Mazel spoke up.

"Raven, don't. They might have poisoned it."

"How do you know?" I asked.

"Raven, you do not accept food from a demon without their blessing. It's like their number one rule, down here. Every time you have eaten with Lucifer, he has given you his blessing in some way, shape, or form. For instance, he'll say, 'enjoy' or 'hope you enjoy your meal'."

"But I'm hungry," I whine. "I haven't eaten in about a day."

"Fine, whatever. Poison yourself. I don't care."

"But you do care, Mazel," I said, smiling.

"How do you figure?"

"If you didn't care, you would not have warned me. Only someone who cares about a person, warns them before they get hurt."

"Whatever," she said.

"Why didn't they bring you food?" I asked.

"Are you that stupid? Do you not know what demons eat?"

"Know that you have asked that, I am assuming I don't know."

"We feast on souls, flesh, blood. Ever heard of the term, drink the blood of our enemies? We're the ones who started that saying. Anything else we eat is empty to us. It does us no good to eat them."

"Oh. When was the last time you ate?" I cautiously asked.

"Don't worry about it. It wasn't too long ago, though."

"That is...that's...Mazel? I-I-don't feel so well." I started to get light-headed as a sharp pain, hit me.

I yelled out, as I twisted my body.

"Raven? Are you alright? Raven! Answer me!" Mazel screamed. "Help!" Mazel yelled. "We need help in here."

Someone opened the cell and unlocked my chains, I fell forward and screamed.

Iron Cage

When I woke up, I was so tired. I could barely keep my eyes open, so I closed them. I don't know what happened to me. I just...everything happened so fast. One minute I was changed up, the next minute I'm screaming in pain. "What is happening to me?" I ask aloud. This isn't the first time that this has happened. It seems like I have been feeling worse by the day. I first started to feel bad after my first day in Hell. Maybe I'm coming down with some kind of virus?

"Good. You're finally awake," Caleb said, coming into my view. "Hope you're comfortable."

I started to notice my surroundings. I was sitting in a metal chair, with my hands tied behind the back of the chair. I stretched my fingers out and could feel wires that were tied to the chair. I looked over to my right and saw a huge tank with an iron cage suspended over the tank. "What the heck?"

"Ah," Caleb gave me a toothy grin. "You don't have to worry about the water, as long as you cooperate with me. Okay?"

"Why am I tied up?"

"Even though Lucifer won't admit it, you are stronger than you look. With the blood of two angel's running through your veins, you are a creature no one has ever even seen. Heck, after this is all over, I might keep you for myself. At least here, you'll be happier."

"What are you talking about?" I ask. "I am happy with Lucifer. He treats me right and he doesn't tie me up against my will."

"Raven, darling, you are so funny. You are not here against your own will," Caleb smiled at me.

"Then let me go."

"No. You're my guest. How about this: I'll let you go once you tell me everything I want to know."

"But I don't know anything. I just got here."

"You do know things. Now, I do not want to spend all day arguing with-" Screams interrupted Caleb. He smiled when they got louder. "Looks like your friend, Maze, got a question wrong."

"Why are you doing this?" I cried. Mazel's screams were getting to me and honestly, I wanted them to stop, one way or another.

"Raven, darling, I'm a demon. I'm in Hell for a reason. I might as well, make my time here, worth-while."

"But-"

"No more comments, questions, or concerns." Caleb snapped his fingers and a guy I've never seen before walked in pushing a cart full of sharp tools. Caleb clapped his hands together in a childish manner and smiled. "Now, shall we begin?"

Drowning. I'm going to drown. He's finally going to kill me this time. Thirty-one. Thirty-two. Thirty-three. I struggle, in the cage, slowly drowning in the freezing water. I had no room to move, the cage outlining my body, pressing up against it. My lungs were burning, screaming for oxygen. Thirty-four. Thirty-five. Thirty-six.

This iron body-molded prison is where I was going to die. I had never been claustrophobic or even feared drowning, but at this moment I was suffering from both fears and losing.

Thirty-seven. Thirty-eight. Thirty-nine. Forty. My limbs start to feel really heavy as my body goes numb. I stopped struggling in the iron prison. I was so weak and there seemed to be no point in fighting anyway.

I opened my mouth to let out what little air might have been in my lungs. My muscles relaxed, and I felt calm for that moment. Everything started to go black.

Forty-one. Forty-two. For-

In that moment the cage was lifted from the water. I started choking up water and gasping for air. My lungs greedily took in the oxygen, and I started crying.

Caleb snapped his fingers and two guys entered the room and walked over to the cage. They undid the lock and I fell back into the water. They both grabbed my arms and pulled my weak body out. Caleb walked over to the table and grabbed something. I watched as he slipped the shiny item in between his knuckles. He, then, walked back to the center of the room.

They carried my body over to Caleb and dropped me at his feet and left the room.

"I hope you had a nice swim," Caleb laughed.

"Why are you doing this? What have I ever done to you?" I asked as I gathered enough strength to stand up. I have known Caleb for a really long time, or so I thought. I always thought he was a nice geeky boy.

"Raven," Caleb laughed again, "you never really know a person until you get down to their personal Hell and spend some time with them."

"I did like you in Raven, I really did. I still do. If you tell me where the dagger is, I'll let you go for the night. I just need the dagger for some personal business."

I shook my head, shivering. "I don't understand."

Sighing, Caleb pulled his fist back. "I don't want you to understand, I want you to feel." Caleb brought his fist down on my face.

Pain exploded in my face as my head was thrown left. Blood sprayed from my mouth and splattered on the floor. I fell to the ground, cradling my face.

"Raven," Caleb sighed again, grabbing a fist-full of my hair and yanking me upwards. "You must have seen it. Lucifer trusts you more than he has ever trusted anyone else. Just tell me where the Ambreison Dagger is, and I'll quit for the night, I promise."

"How do I know I can trust you?" I growled, blood dripping down my face.

"We, demons, can't lie. We can deviate from the truth, but we can't straight out lie. Plus, once a demon makes a promise, they can't break it."

"I don't know what you're talking about," I cried. "Please, just let me go."

"Raven, Raven, Raven. Darling, you know I can't do that. Until you tell me what I want to know. I will say this though: you are not an easy person to crack. Now, I know you know where this dagger is, so I am going to ask you one more time. Please, I strongly urge you to tell. Me. The. Truth. Failure to do so, well, let's just say that you won't like it." He winked at me.

"You're sick."

"So, what? I am who I am, buttercup," he yanked my head sideways.

"When Lucifer gets ahold of you I am going to make sure that he personally makes the rest of your days down here a living Hell," I yelled. I don't know how well that threat would hold up, but it was the only thing I could think to say in that moment.

That seemed to be the wrong thing to say because Caleb growled and pulled his fist back and with all his might, he brought his fist down on my face.

The Clue

I was hot. Everything around me was so hot. I was no longer in the room that I currently resided in my current situation.

I looked around in a room that looked familiar. The walls were lined with bookcases and there was a desk in the room and two doors. Wait! This is Lucifer's study. How did I get here? I asked myself. The room was trashed. Papers and books scattered everywhere on the floor, pictures knocked off the walls, onto the floor. There seemed to even be scorch marks on the walls and ceiling.

What the Hell happened here? I question. It looked like someone threw a fit in here.

A knock on the door startled me.

"Come in," a hoarse voice said from the corner of the room.

Leven entered the room with Anthony and two other people.

"Any news?"

"No, Master Lucifer, she has yet to be found. Mazel is still missing too."

"Then what are you all doing in my study?" Lucifer asked, remaining in the shadows where we could not see him.

"We came to tell you that all signs point to Caleb and the kidnappings. We have yet to find where he is keeping the girls', but we know that it was definitely him."

"How do you know this?" Lucifer quietly asked.

"Lillian Liizel saw that he has the girls, but she can't find any clues that would tell us where they're being held."

"This should not have happened," Lucifer whispered. "I should have been watching her. I'll never forgive myself if anything happens to Raven. Leave me. I want to be alone."

"You sure that is wise? You haven't fed since she left which was three days-" Leven started.

"Get out," Lucifer whispered.

"But sir, you really should-"

"Shut the fuck up and get the Hell out!" Lucifer yelled, jumping out from the shadows.

"Holy-" One of the guards started but quickly shut up and ran out of the room when Lucifer threw a fireball at him.

Everyone scurried out of the room, leaving me with him.

Lucifer looked horrible. The sparkle in his eyes was gone, replaced by dark circles. His black hair was a greasy mess, his clothes had holes in them, I could only guess from scorch marks. I can't really tell but I am sure he probably smelt bad too.

"Raven, I know you can't hear me, but I am so sorry. I'm sorry I yelled at you and I am sorry to have brought you down here. Who knows what Caleb is doing to you at this moment. I swear, I will not rest until I find you and I will end him... permanently."

My body at that moment started to hurt. I gasped as I doubled over.

Lucifer walked over to his desk and picked up a skull and looked at it. "Raven, why the Hell did I let you go? Why?!" He screamed as he threw the skull in my direction.

I dodged as it sped past me. Lucifer sat in his chair that was behind his desk and put his head in his hands.

"Lucifer, please hurry," I plead as the pain in my body starts to increase. I walked to his desk. Once I reached him, I reached out to touch him. To my surprise, my hand rested on his shoulder. This gave me an idea. Leaning over, closer to him, I whispered in his ear, "Please find me."

Lucifer lifted his head so fast that I jumped back. "Raven?"

Tears started to fill my eyes as I smiled, "Can you hear me?"

"Raven," Lucifer called out. "Can you hear me? Can you give me a sign? Can you tell me where you are?"

My heart dropped when I realized that he couldn't hear me. To make matters worse, the pain started to spread throughout my body. Something told me that I didn't have much time.

Frantically, I searched my mind to find clues that could help Lucifer find me. All I remember is waking up in a dungeon. It was dark and cold. The floors- No! Raven, that won't help him. Think! Is there anything you remember before they took you to the dungeon?

I started to cry when I realized I couldn't remember anything. All remember is Lucifer's study, being knocked out. I remember waking up before I was brought to the dungeon. Wait! That's it! I woke up before I was brought to the dungeon. I searched my mind to remember exactly what I saw outside. I saw the building, it was run down. It sort of looked like one of those old abandoned mansions. I couldn't get a better description because they realized I was awake and knocked me out.

That's it! I just need to find something that I can use to clue in Lucifer. I look around the room for anything I could use to tell him where I was at. Maybe I could draw a picture of a mansion? No, that wouldn't do. I can't draw. Maybe a...a book!

I ran over to his bookshelf and looked for the book I saw when I first explore his study room. It was a book called 'The Fall of the House of Usher' by Edgar Allen Poe. That mansion in the book sort of reminded me of the mansion we are in right now.

Quickly, I searched for the book and started to panic when I couldn't find the book on his bookshelf. A pain so sharp, brought me to my knees. The pain was too much and I laid on the floor, crying.

My vision started to fade, and I knew my time was up. I looked over towards Lucifer, who looked around the room, frantically.

A book caught my eye as I looked back down towards the ground. The book that I was looking for was just out of my reach. I gathered what little strength I had left and crawled over to the book. I grabbed the book and with all my might, I flung the book across the room. As soon as it landed in front of Lucifer's desk, pain exploded in my stomach and I passed out.

I woke up screaming as Caleb had the Katondra to my stomach.

"Oh goody. You're awake," Caleb smiled as he turned off the weapon. "I am so glad that you have decided to come back to us."

"I wish I could say the same thing," I hoarsely replied, shivering. I looked around to find myself in the same room as I was in before I passed out. This time, however, I was strapped to the same chair I was in before I was put into the iron cage.

Caleb snapped his fingers and one of his bodyguards brought him a bucket of water. Caleb grabbed the bucket and flung the water on me, which caused me to shiver even more.

"What was that for?" I yelled.

"I think I may have been a little too soft on you before. Almost drowning doesn't seem to scare you but let's see how electrocution does for you." He grinned evilly as he walked over to a panel on the wall.

Pain

"How about we start out with a question that is simple?" Caleb smiled.

"What do you want to know?" I growled.

Caleb had switched places with one of his bodyguards, who took his position next to the table by the wall. Caleb unstrapped me from the chair and had me chained to the wall. He then had another chair brought into the room, which he placed right in front of me.

"When you were given the choice to choose the fate of the world, why did you choose both?"

"How did I know that someone who really hates me would ask me that question?" I asked, rolling my eyes. I was starting to get uncomfortable in the chair, but I couldn't move because he still had me tied to the chair.

Caleb laughed and asked, "What makes you think that I hate you?"

"Oh. I'm sorry. Were all your different techniques of torture how you treat people you like? I am so sorry, I completely misjudged your methods."

"Well, you were given a choice of the easy or hard way. You chose the hard way. Raven, you grew up practically alone with no one to teach you right and wrong. How are you going to learn unless someone teaches you?"

"I know right from wrong. For example, I know that what you are doing is actually wrong."

Caleb and his bodyguard burst out laughing. I gave him a confused look. "Darling, you're in Hell. What I am doing is actually very acceptable. In fact, it is what we do down here. We are down here to learn from our mistakes and to make the dead suffer for what they did in their previous life."

"But I didn't do anything wrong! I am not even dead!" I yelled.

"That is where you are wrong, my dear. You chose to live with Lucifer and you denied God. That itself will send you straight to Hell once you die. You should have chosen to live in Heaven rather than Hell. You will eventually pay for your choice."

"What do you mean I will pay for my choice? I regret nothing."

"Oh, but you will," Caleb smiled. "You are going to answer me what I want to know, or I am going to make you hurt really, really, bad."

"But I don't know anything!' I yelled.

"We'll see how much you really know," Caleb laughed.

"Raven, I am starting to get tired of you not being obedient. Just answer the damn questions and you are free for the night." Caleb punched me in the face.

Crying, I whispered, "I have known Micheal for as long as I can remember. I think I first met him when I was eight, maybe nine. I can't remember. I do not know that he has any weaknesses."

My whole body was sore. Every time I would answer a question in a way that Caleb disliked, he would punch me somewhere on my body. The most common place for him to punch me was the face. Occasionally, he would punch me in the stomach multiple times.

"Why did you follow Mazel into the study room?"

"I heard her scream, so I naturally ran into the room," I answered.

Caleb made a buzzer noise, "Wrong answer. We both know that she didn't scream out." Caleb snapped his fingers and his guard brought over some wires that had metal squares at the end of them.

"Oh, please," I started to plead. I knew exactly what those were for. "No, please don't." I cried as the guard ripped off my shirt, exposing my black bra.

Caleb laughed, as the guard put the wires all over my body. "I'm starting to think that you have a kink to pain, Raven."

I tried to save my butt by responding, "I followed her into the room because I was talking to her before she walked into the study."

"You're too late, Raven. You cannot answer whenever you feel like answering. You need to be trained." Caleb nodded at the guard. "Put it on one."

Raven, don't scream, don't show any signs he's getting to you. You are a strong lady who can handle pain.

I thought if I coached myself I could mentally prepare myself for what was coming.

I watched as the guard flipped the switch. At first, I felt nothing at all. Then the guard walked over to the desk and sat down. I saw him mess with some switches and dials and then he moved a lever up one notch.

That's when I felt it. I felt the electricity coursing through my body, reaching every single part of my body. Even though the electricity was on low, it still really hurt. My mental prep did nothing to help me. The electrical shock hit my body in all the places at once. A scream formed in my throat and I pursed my lips together to keep the scream from coming out. I did not want to give him the satisfaction that I was actually hurting.

Caleb stared at me as I forced myself not to scream. "Come on, Raven, we both know that you are in pain. Just give into the pain and give me a little scream. I want to see those pretty little lips move in pain."

I shook my head, tears rolling down my face. I was not going to scream. I could handle this pain.

Growling, Caleb nodded at the guard, "Crank it up to two."

Nodding, the guard pushed the lever up one more notch.

All at once, my body felt like it was on fire. My body involuntarily started jerking. The pain was so great that I bit my tongue to try to cancel out the pain from the shock. It wasn't working as much as I wanted it to.

I whimpered as the tears started to flow faster. I changed tactics and bit the inside of my cheek. I bit down so hard, blood started to flow.

Caleb walked closer to me and shook his head. He then punched me in the stomach and I lost all my willpower to keep my mouth shut.

I let out the loudest scream I have ever heard. It was so loud that Caleb actually flinched.

Finally, the electricity is shut off. I gasped with relief, coughing violently.

With a smile on his face, Caleb pulled up a chair. "Now," he started as he sat down in his chair, "it's starting to become fun."

?

Adam's First Wife

By the time Caleb figured I have had enough, I was coughing up blood. Blood from screaming in so much pain and everything else he did to me. I am pretty sure something inside me has been liquified.

"I have to admit, Raven, you are pretty impressive. I have tortured a bunch of humans, demons, and even some angels and I have to say you are probably one of the strongest creatures I have ever had the pleasure of torturing," Caleb bowed his head in some sort of respectful way.

"I honestly," I started, grimacing at the pain in my chest, "do not know what to say to that."

"Don't say anything, just listen," Caleb instructed. "Now, I know, after putting you through a couple of my favorite ways to torture people, you are pretty stubborn. I have come to the conclusion that you either know the answers I am seeking and you're very good with concealing them, or you actually don't know anything. Either way, with this observation, I have a hypothesis. You may not be talking now but after I show you what is behind the black screen of this television," he points to the far right corner of the room where the device was, "you might and will change your mind."

I gather the strength to laugh, which causes me to grimace, once again. "Even if I knew anything, which I don't, what makes you think that I will change my mind?"

"Raven," Caleb walked closer to me, a collar in his hand, "my beautiful darling Raven. Did you forget I have known you for about ten years? I know what makes you tick. Even though you acted all tough, pretending you don't care about people, I knew better. Even though you distant yourself from everyone, you craved a friend but you could never allow yourself to have a friend. Sure, you have Michael, but honestly, you knew something was different about him from the start. The thing is, Raven, you never really got emotionally attached to anyone because of your fear."

"And what fear are you referring to?" I asked him.

"The fear that if you start caring for someone again, they might be ripped from your life, once more, like your parents were," He responded, putting the collar around me.

"That's not-"

"Not true? Of course, you would say that. Confirming it would allow others, like me, to use that weakness against you. I want to test something. Let me ask you a sincere question. On a scale of one to ten, how much do you care for Mazel?"

I didn't exactly know where this was going, but I knew that I would not like it. My heart started to race and I forced myself to remain calm. "Who says I even care for her? She tried to kill me when I first entered this world, you know."

Smiling, Caleb rubbed his hands together. "Great! Then you should mind watching this." He nodded to the guy in the room who flipped a switch.

On the screen of the T.V. was Mazel, but I barely recognized her. Her appearance completely surprised me. They had shaved her head, which made her look like a total badass. If I had met her when her head was shaved, I never would have messed with her in the first place. Given the current situation, however, she did not look like a badass. She looked like a scared woman who was beaten and was covered in blood from head-to-toe.

Mazel was sitting in the corner, in a pool of her own blood. She had her knees pulled up to her chest and her arms rested on top of them. I noticed that she didn't have chains around her arms. Instead, she had a chain that wrapped around her stomach.

"What in the world did you do to her?" I asked. "Why did you shave her head?"

"We shaved her head because shaving a female's hair is like stripping away a part of their identity. Wouldn't you agree? Without your hair, what would you be? Nothing. Besides, she's a demon, she can handle a little pain or in her case, a lot."

Caleb nodded to the guy at the table who told some guys to enter the room. "You all may proceed."

Five guys walked into the room. Two of them picked Mazel up and held her arms tight. Two of them stood on either side of her while the last one stood in front of her with what looked like a brander. This guy had a scar running down the left side of his face. His left eye sewn shut.

"What are you planning on doing to her?"

"Whatever I need to do in order to get some information out of her or you," Caleb said simply. "Go ahead."

The guy with the brand didn't give Mazel any warning as he plunged the hot iron against her stomach. Mazel let out a cry that made me cringe so bad. "Please!" she yelled, "I have told you everything I know."

Scarface pulled the brander away from her stomach and inspected his work. I could see on the screen her bloody brand. It looked like two J's put side by side, one of them backward. "You now belong to me," he smiled at her as he walked out of the room, satisfied.

Caleb walked over to the table and pressed a button. His voice came up over the intercom. "You really want to give me that line, Lilith," Caleb spat. "Come on! You are almost as old as this dumb planet. You were there when God created that stupid tool!"

"I. Don't. Know. Where. It. Is." Mazel sneered.

"You know what? I was hoping we could avoid this but I guess there is no other option. Boys, get the Dagger." Caleb turned to the guy at the table. "Hizel, keep the intercom on. I want Mazel to hear this," Caleb turned to me.

"You want to know something interesting? Did you know that Adam had a wife before Eve? Her name was Lilith. God had created her out of the same earth he created Adam. She was cast from the Garden of Eden because she wouldn't be subservient to Adam. You know how they say that God is perfect and he makes no mistakes? Well, meet exhibit A. Here is Adam's first wife. The thing is, God made her have too much love. Then he got mad when she didn't turn out just as he had planned."

"I have never heard of this before," I told Caleb.

"That's because people these days try to hide the truth. They don't want others to know that God made a mistake when he made her. Now, the thing is, since she wasn't allowed in the Garden of Eden, he gave her a special mission, if you will. He made it her mission to spread the love on

Earth. Ever heard of the Goddess Aphrodite? Well, where do you think her story came from? This chick right here. The thing is, however, is that even though she was cast from the Garden, she was still considered an angel at one time. Which means she has wings. We'll get back to that in a minute.

"Now, if you read the Bible, or listen to the stories, God created man and woman to love the opposite. That was his intention for humankind. Fast forward to a couple thousand years after Lilith was created, comes her biggest act of all. Guess where homosexuals come from? That's right. Lilith thought it would be funny if she made two guys fall in love.

"God, furious, stripped her of her title and cursed her to never feel love for as long as she exists. To never truly be satisfied and once she died she would go straight to Hell where she will live out the rest of her life out, miserable, alone, and never loved."

An Angel with No Wings

"**S**ir, we got the dagger," one of the people said as he entered the room where Mazel was at.

"Oh, goody!" Caleb clapped. "I just finished my story."

"Now, back to the wings. Since she was once an angel, if you will, she has wings. Have you ever seen her wings?"

"N-no," I whispered. I knew where this was going.

"Well, you're about to see them. I have to say, they are really pretty. I'm surprised God let her keep them after he announced she was Fallen. That means she's no longer allowed in Heaven."

"What are you going to do to her?" I asked.

"Oh, Raven, you know exactly what I'm going to do," Caleb laughed. "Go ahead. Do whatever you can to get the wings out. When they are out, get the medicine ready," Caleb instructed.

I watched on the screen as they punched, cut, branded, and even shot at her. She screamed each time they drew blood.

"The thing is, Raven, Mazel or Lilith here, can actually withstand a lot of pain. It is one of the benefits for having angel blood coursing through her body. Yes, it may be tainted now, but it's still there. You and her are not so different. Well, I guess you are. You are something no one has ever seen, not even God. So, you have to excuse us all if we want to cut you open and see what makes you tick."

"Lucifer would never let you do that," I whispered, horrified. I knew he would cut me up, given the chance.

"Lucifer doesn't fucking care about you!" Caleb screamed in my face. "If he cared about you he wouldn't let me be doing what I am doing to you!" Caleb grabbed a fistful of my hair and punched me in the side of the head. I yelled out as pain exploded in my head. I was still chained to the wall and when he punched me, my head hit the back of the wall so hard that I heard something crack. A few seconds later I felt something warm oozing down the back of my neck.

"You're a worthless bitch," Caleb spat as he released my hair. "I honestly don't know why he chose you. You're nothing!"

"You know," I hissed, as I struggled to see. My vision was blurry and my head was in so much pain. "I hope, when Lucifer comes, and he will, he tears you to shred."

"Lucifer is not going to do shit. You want to know why? That bitch is too emotional right now that he is not even eating. That's right. He's refused to eat until your body is found. Did you know that it has been three days since I've kidnapped you? Three days and the dude is getting weaker by the minute. It's all part of the plan. Kidnap you and the dagger. Once Lucifer is too weak to fight because he's all worried about you, I will kill him without even thinking. It's perfect, actually." Caleb laughed manically.

"You're-" I started to say he was crazy but then we both heard a scream. We both look up at the screen just in time to see Mazel's grey wings explode from her back. That's when chaos erupted. The two guys that held her arm went flying as soon as her wings came out. Growling, she turned so abruptly that one of her wings cut the other guy that was standing to the left of her.

His left arm went flying as he fell to the ground. Blood started pouring from the wound of his missing arm. I gagged and forced myself not to throw up at the scene. I have never seen anything like it before.

Everyone in the room was screaming trying to get her to calm down.

"Sedate that bitch!" Caleb kept yelling as she threw his people across the wall. He called for more backup as soon as Mazel killed three of his guys.

Seven more people ran into the room. Two guys kicked behind her knee and she went down. Quickly, they open the chains that are on the ground and lock her legs in it. Instantly, everyone does their best to hold her down. It took two guys to hold each arm. It took two guys to hold each wing. Then, in front of her stood Scarface with a syringe that had a long needle. He put the needle aside long enough to get a chain and clasp it around her neck.

Mazel roared as she struggled to get free. Even with her incredible strength, she failed. Then Scarface instructed the guys holding her wings to pull them apart so he could reach the middle of her back. Without warning, he plunged the needle in between her shoulder blades and released whatever fluid was in the tube. Instantly, I could see her wings go limp.

"What did you put in her?" I asked.

"Some sort of anesthetic, if you will. The thing is, Raven, it's not a numbing agent for her body; just her wings. She will be able to feel every little bit that is about to happen."

"What-" I looked up at the screen and saw Scarface hold a serrated saw. "Oh my God! You can't do this!" I yelled as I tried to get out of my restraints. "Let me out of these chains!" I yelled.

Caleb just laughed as he told the guy to proceed. Scarface nodded and held the saw at the top of her right wing. Slowly, he pushed the saw down in to the wing. Mazel screamed as blood started pouring from her back.

"Please!" she screamed. "I told you everything I know. Please don't do this!" She tried to pull out of everyone's grip but wasn't strong enough. I watched her as she tried to free her wings but her wings were too drugged up to move.

"Too late," Caleb said, over the intercom. "We already started."

I watched, horrified as Scarface laughed as Mazel's screams got louder. He seemed to be enjoying it and so did Caleb.

Scarface was halfway done and I could see that the fire in Mazel was burning out quickly. She had stopped fighting but was still screaming.

How could someone do something so horrendous and not even care? I couldn't take it anymore. I could barely breathe. All the noises around me faded as my heart started racing and my head started to spin. My vision was fading in and out. What is happening to me? "Okay!" I yelled. "I lied. I do care about her. Please stop. Just stop it!"

Caleb just looked at me and laughed. "Shut and watch the show," he growled. "I am done giving you both chances, Raven. No more going easy anymore. You think you're safe? I know that you have wings too and if I have to, I will have yours cut off too."

"You don't have to do this! We don't know. We really don't. What more do you want from us? From me?"

"Oh, Raven, I want a lot of things from you. A lot of things that I intend to get once this is all said and done. By the time I am done with you, Lucifer isn't going to want you. You will be so damaged, so scarred and ruined that he will see you and think that you are worthless. You'll just be another person living here. Nothing special."

"That's not-"

"Not true? Oh come on, Raven!" Caleb slammed his fist into the wall next to my head. "Lucifer doesn't give a fuck about you! How many times am I going to have to tell you? He doesn't fucking care! You are just another tool for him to use and once he is done with you, you will be tossed aside; just like he did with Mazel."

"I refuse to believe that...he...Lucifer..." I fell silent as the room started to spin again. I closed my eyes and took deep breaths. Finally, the room stopped spinning and all the noises returned.

Caleb looked up at the screen and smiled. "There you have it ladies and gentlemen: An angel with no wings."

I looked up at the screen and gasped, horrified. The guards had released her from their grasp and she was lying on the ground, wailing. Blood pooled around her and soaked the white wraps around her body. She raised her head up and reached out to touch her wings. "They're gone. They're gone. My wings. My beautiful wings. They took them. They're just...gone." Her wailing got louder and louder.

The guards were leaving the room, when Caleb yelled, "Shut her up!"

Scarface smiled and walked up to Mazel. Lifting her up from the ground he pulled out his serrated saw.

"No!" I yelled as I watched him cut her throat. Mazel's wailing stopped and he threw her body against the wall. She laid on the ground, blood gushing not only from her back but her throat. I could hear her choking on her own blood.

"I'm going to kill you," I whispered under my breath, enraged. Something inside me started to boil. I don't know if it was adrenaline or just pure rage but something started to boil and I wanted to taste his blood.

"What?" Caleb asked with an entertained look on his face. "What did you say?"

"I said I am going to fucking kill you!" I screamed, twisting and turning, trying to free myself from the chains that kept me a prisoner to the wall. I could feel them loosening up. "I'm going to kill you for all the torture you have put us through! Once I get the chance, I will kill you. I will cut out your heart and I will set it on fire. I will set this entire place on fire." With one final tug, the wall behind me exploded, concrete flying everywhere, as I broke free from my chains.

Standing up, I let out a demonic scream as I rushed towards Caleb. "I am going to fucking kill you!"

Caleb picked up a remote from the table next to him and smiled. "I don't think so," he said when I was a few feet from him. "Say goodnight, Princess," he smirked as he pressed a button.

Pain exploded in my head and I fell to the ground, screaming. Caleb's manic laughter is the last thing I remember before I passed out.

Forever Branded

When I first opened my eyes, I winced. It was so bright outside compared to where I was right now. All around me, little children were playing on the play grounds. They were laughing and squealing with joy as they took turns down the slide, as they chased each other around, as they talked to each other. Their parents stood close by to them, talking to other parents, while eyeing their children.

"It's pretty. Isn't it?" A voice beside asked.

"Mom!" I cried, as I threw my arms around her. "I've missed you so much!"

"I've missed you too, Angel. Your dad told me to tell you hello and that he misses you so very much," she said, releasing from the hug.

"I miss him too. I must ask, though, what are you doing here?" I asked.

"What do you mean? I live here. This is my home."

I gasped and tears started to form in my eyes. "Am I...am I dead?"

"No, Angel, you are not dead, but I have to say, you are not far from it. What Caleb is doing to you is horrific."

"If you can see what is happening to us, why can't you help?"

"Raven, honey, we angels, cannot interfere with business in Hell. We would not even survive if we stepped foot on grounds that is tainted in blood, death, and sin. We are too holy for that," Mom explained.

"So, you're just going to let me die here?" I cried.

"Raven, we can't do anything to help you. I am so sorry. None of this would have happened if you had chosen to live in Heaven with your dad and I," she said, walking away from me.

"What do you mean, none of this would have never happened?" I asked, my voice rising. "You told me the last time we met that I should make sure I make the right choice. I did."

Shaking her head, she stopped walking. "Why did you choose both? Why didn't you just choose good? Why let evil live in this world?"

"Mom, you of all people should understand. Where would we be if we existed in a world with only good?"

"We would be in a better place, I know that much," she said.

"True, but in a world with just good, people would never know what it means to be grateful for anything. They would never know what it means to struggle. They would never know loss. Now, in a world with all evil, people would never know hope. They would never know what love is. They would never know that times will get better. You can't just live in a world with one or the other. You need a balance."

Before she could speak, I continued. "Think of it like this, Mom: you can't have a yin without a yang. In this world, people need both the sun and the moon. Without both, no one can survive. Without both good and evil, living on this planet is worthless."

My mom just stood shaking her head. I thought she was going to yell when instead she started crying. "I am so sorry that I brought you to the park that day. If we hadn't of, you would have grown up with us."

"Mom, you can't change the past. Besides, everything happens for a reason. This, this horrible event I'm going through right now is happening for a reason...I am sure of it."

"Raven, my Angel, you are so smart." My mom hugged me, burying her face in my hair. After a few seconds, I heard her crying.

"What's wrong?" I asked, not letting her go.

"Promise me, Raven. Promise me whatever you do you will not give up. You will fight until your dying breath. You will show anyone who ever stands in your way who the boss is. Promise me!" she yelled, pulling away from me.

"I promise. What-" Then an invisible force ripped her away from me. Our surrounding started to change. The world started to darken and people started to disappear.

"Raven!" she screamed as she was pulled farther and farther away from me.

"Mom!" I yelled, starting to run after her. In that moment, chains exploded from the ground and wrapped around my legs. "Mom! Mom! Please come back!" Chains instantly appeared around my arms.

"Raven!" my mom yelled her voice very far away. "Just remember you fight until you can't fight no more."

"Mom! Mom! Please don't leave me. Mom! Come back!" I screamed. "I promise. I do," I cried as the last bit of the peaceful world around me disappeared.

I woke up with a gasp. The first thing I saw when I opened my eyes was Caleb standing right in front of me with a huge smile on his face. "Auntie Em! Auntie Em! Please come back, Auntie Em." He mocked and then laughed. "Nightmare, Princess?"

"None of your business," I spat. I looked around the room and saw Mazel still on the floor. For a second I thought she was dead, but then I saw her stir in her sleep. Poor Mazel, I thought to myself. She has suffered more than I have. Turning back to Caleb I asked him, "Why am I tied up again? Haven't you tortured us enough?"

With the biggest smile, I have ever seen Caleb with, he responded, "Nope. My dear Princess, I haven't. When you were out, I thought of something. I need to sign my work. You saw what Jackson did to Mazel. That was his masterpiece. That was his cattle. I gave him an all-access pass to do whatever he wanted to her. You, however, are my cattle. I am your master and I will sign my work of art."

"Why?" I asked, trying to keep the fear from being so obvious.

"Let's just say," Caleb snapped his fingers and in walked Scarface with a brander, "for some crazy reason, I happen to show mercy and let you out of here. I don't want you to forget what happened to you here. I don't want to be another memory you cast aside. I will be forever branded into your mind and skin."

"You won't. I promise," I said, quickly. I watched Scarface touch the end of the brander and the iron heat up.

"Nah, you will, Raven. You will try. With this brand, however, you can never truly be rid of me. I will be with you forever." Caleb grabbed the brand away from Scarface and smiled. "I just have one question before I begin: Which is your dominant side?" Scarface slipped out of the room, almost unnoticed.

Without thinking, I blurted out, "My left side."

"Perfect," Caleb said, smiling. "I can't wait to see how you will fight with your dominant side messed up."

Before I could question him, he quickly pressed the hot iron against my skin, on my left shoulder. My body, no stranger to pain, cried out in pain. I had to bite my tongue, hard, to keep from screaming. The room started to smell like burning flesh and it was nauseating. I wanted to throw up. After a few more seconds with the hot iron against my skin, Caleb pulled it away and inspected his work.

"It's actually one of the best signatures I've ever done." He smiled at his work.

I turned my head to look at my shoulder. There was a straight line that ran vertically. Then two parallel lines ran horizontally on that line. At the bottom of the symbol was an infinity sign. "Now, you will never be rid of me. With this mark, you are branded for all of eternity," Caleb cackled. At that moment, Scarface walked into the room with a tray of food. He set the tray on the ground.

"Release her," Caleb commanded Scarface. Scarface listened released me from my chains. I fell to the ground with a thud. "Better get your strength up Princess. You're going to need it. I decided to let you fight for your freedom."

My heart started to race in hope. "If you win, you both are free to go."

"If I lose?" I asked.

"If you lose...Well, let's just say that I'll own you for the rest of your life," Caleb responded with a hungry look in his eye.

Choosing a Weapon

"**M**azel," I shook Mazel, hoping I could wake her up. "Mazel, please wake up. I need you."

Mazel did not stir. Fear started to well up in me as I tried to find a pulse on Mazel. She didn't seem to be breathing. That was when the tears started to flow. I threw myself over Mazel's body and cried.

"I am so sorry, Mazel. I am so sorry. This is all my fault. If I hadn't stopped you in the- No. I'm glad I stopped you from killing yourself. There are so many things I wanted to tell you but I can't. If you were here, I would tell you that even though you tried to kill me when I first arrived, I am so glad that I met you. Caleb was right: I am so afraid to let people in my life because I don't want to lose anyone else. I lost my mom and dad and now I have lost you. I am so sorry." I was crying so hard I could no longer talk. I just stayed hunched over Mazel's body and cried.

"Bitch, get off of me before I roast your ass," Mazel whispered, hoarsely as she tried to push me away from her.

"Oh my God! You're alive!" I cried. "I thought you were dead."

"You're so fucking dramatic," Mazel glared at me. "Help me sit up."

I quickly, but very carefully helped Mazel sit up. I was careful not to touch her back. "Mazel, I don't know if you heard Caleb but he is giving me a chance to fight for our freedom."

Mazel looked at me in disbelief. "You're kidding me, right?"

"No, he said if I win he'll let us both go. But if I lose he'll kill you and keep me for the rest of my life."

"Well, shit. We're screwed then." When I started to protest, Mazel held up her hand. "Listen, I'm not going to lie to you. You are not the best fighter. When you fought Zaphara, you almost killed yourself. No offense, Princess, but if our lives depend on you, I might as well be dead."

"But what about what Lucifer said about my wings? Can't I use them like you did to fight off-" I stopped talking because we both knew how it ended with her wings.

"Yeah, a lot of good that did me, Princess. They cut out my fucking wings. They're gone and I'm never getting them back. The only thing that re-minded me that I was once an angel is now gone. Now, I am nothing. So, yeah, go ahead and use your wings. Don't go and blame me when they rip your wings out too."

"Mazel, please, I need your help. I am supposed to be something special with unknown abilities but I don't even know what I can do. If I can learn to use my wings, I might be able to stand a chance."

Mazel sighed and shook her head. "Listen, Princess, and I mean listen well. I know you think that you have a chance to defeat Caleb, but you can't. No one can. Well, Lucifer can but he's not here and he's not coming. I'm going to tell you something that I've never told anyone before. Just let me die. I don't deserve to live anymore.

"My one regret in my life is the fact that I never could get anyone to love me. I once loved Lucifer but he doesn't love me and never will. So why should I try anymore? I know I haven't known you for long but I do know this. You will fight Caleb with everything you have, and I hate to say this but you will most likely fail unless some miracle happens. I want you to know, if you fail, I don't blame you for anything that has happened to me. My time was coming to an end and I have accepted it. You know how they say that Karma's a bitch? Well, I'm bitchier and if I have to die, I want you to know that I am glad I'm not dying alone."

"Mazel, I don't-"

The door to the cell opened and in walked Caleb and Scarface. "Time's up, dear. You ready to fight for your freedom?"

"Not really, but let's get this over with," I sighed.

Smiling Caleb grabbed my arm and motioned to Scarface to grab Mazel. "Well then, let's go to the fight room. I hope you are prepared to lose."

"The rules are quite simple," Caleb started as one of his servants finished strapping the armor to my body. "Do whatever you can to win. Do you want any weapons?" Caleb motioned to the wall that was covered in weapons from floor to ceiling.

"Yeah," I said as I walked over to the wall. Mazel was sitting next to the wall, strapped to a chair. I gave her a little smile and then I focused my attention back to the wall and I looked for a weapon.

There were so many weapons. Most of them were different types of swords. There were other weapons such as whips, chains, daggers and a few other weapons I do not know of. I carefully scanned the wall, thinking about which weapon would be the best for me. I looked for a Katondra and found one. I reached for it then stopped. Something seemed to call my name as I looked over to the far right of the wall. At the very end were two curved daggers. They had red handles that were covered in weird markings. Without thinking, I grabbed the daggers, spun around, and faced Caleb.

"Raven, wait," Mazel whispered. I looked at Caleb who titled his head in question.

"Give me one minute," I told him then I turned and looked at Mazel. "What?"

"I need you to promuse me that when you need my help, you will let me know. Okay?" she whispered.

"What? How can you help me?"

"Just promise me you will signal me when you need my help," Mazel hissed.

Sighing, I nodded. "I promise." Mazel thanked me and wished me good luck as I turned to face Caleb, once again.

"I'm ready," I said, as I walked to the middle of the room.

Caleb nodded his head and the weapons wall behind me disappeared and was replaced with a regular solid wall.

"Before we begin, let me get changed," Caleb smiled and took a step back and he suddenly began to change. Two horns sprouted from his temples and spiraled upwards about four inches. His skin started to move as if there were bugs lying underneath it. I watched in horror as his skin started to bubble. His once pale skin morphed into colors of red, orange, and black. Red wings popped out from his back and I heard Mazel growl. A reminder of what she once had.

"Now," Caleb spoke, his voice so deep and so loud that it reverberated around the room, "I'm ready to dominate you. I'm so going to enjoy this." Caleb threw his hands to his side and let out a roar. "Let's fight."

Killing Caleb

"Come on!" Caleb yelled. "Make the first move."

I got a better grip on my weapons, as my heart started to pound ferociously in my chest. Without even thinking, I charged towards Caleb.

I pulled the right side of my body back as I raised my left arm, ignoring the searing pain from the brand. Using all my might, I slashed at Caleb's torso, which started to bleed profusely. I raised my hand again to strike him.

Laughing, Caleb caught my hand. He looked down at his torso and I followed his gaze.

"What the-?" I stood there, not pulling away from his grip as I watched the wound heal.

Caleb looked back at me, grinning. With one swift motion, he grabbed my neck and lifted me high above the ground. "You're going to die down here," he declared as he grabbed my daggers from my hands. Then he threw me across the room with such force that I hit the wall and crumbled to the ground.

My body screamed in pain, as I tried to sit up. I could feel the warm liquid from my head, running down my face. I cried out as I attempted to lift my head. I slowly sat up, head pounding.

"Raven, watch out!" Mazel screamed. I looked up just as Caleb threw one of my weapons at me. I tried to move out of the way, but I was too slow. The first dagger hit me on the right shoulder. I screamed out in pain as it connected. I reached up to pull it out of my shoulder as the second dagger hit me under my left rib. Blood started to pour from both of the wounds.

"Come on, Raven. Fight back!" Caleb yelled as he approached me. "No wonder Lucifer isn't looking for you. You're weak as Hell. You're fucking pathetic!"

Gritting my teeth, I pulled both of the daggers out and I stood up. "I," I started as I took one step towards him. "am not pathetic! You are nothing but a fucking cheat. How am I supposed to kill you if you keep healing yourself?" I yelled as I held my daggers in front of me.

Taking a deep breath, I charged towards him. He reached to grab me and quickly, I dropped to my knees. Right before I slid past him, I slashed him in the stomach. Caleb growled as he started to turn around to face me. Without thinking, I stood up and started slashing at his back. Caleb roared as his wing ripped through my stomach.

I fell to the ground in complete agony. I laid on my back as blood started to pool around me.

"It's a shame, really. If only you were taught how to call out your angel when in a fight. Something like that takes a really long time to master." Caleb stood over me and pressed his foot to my chest.

I screamed as I tried to fight him off. I could barely breathe. "I was going to keep you as my pet but I have decided Mazel would be a better pet than your weak ass. So I am left to ask this: any last words?"

"Yeah," I managed to squeak out. "Mazel, now!"

"Wha-" Caleb spun around just in time to see Mazel leap into the air with two long swords.

He threw his hands up to protect his face and Mazel's swords connected with them. His arms fell to the ground. Black blood poured out of the wounds.

"Raven, I need you to think to yourself, chains," Mazel yelled.

Chains? I thought to myself. What-? In that instant, my hands shot in front of me and chains wrapped around Caleb's waist.

"Hold him there!" Mazel yelled. She ran towards me and stood over top of me.

Caleb roared as he tried to break free my chains. I struggled to stay awake as blood kept pouring from my wounds.

Caleb fought to break free from my chains but I held on to him with all my might. Mazel pulled one of his wings out from his back. She lifted her swords high above her head, and in one swift motion, she sliced through his wing.

He roared as he tried to twist out of my grasp. My vision started to fade as I tried to desperately hold Caleb. Caleb twisted around enough to look me in the eyes as he flung one of his bloody stump of an arm in my direction. I screamed when his blood touched my face. It was burning. I released one of my chains from around him as I touched my face to wipe off the blood. Caleb's hands were starting to grow back. I stared at Caleb, horrified as I watched his hands regenerate.

Mazel screamed at me to hold him still as she tried to cut off his other wing. Quickly, I threw my empty hand out towards Caleb and held him still. As quick as lighting, Mazel cut off his other wing. I released him from my chains.

Caleb roared in excruciating pain as he fell to the ground, just a couple of feet away from me. He was breathing really hard as he gurgled up blood. "You know," Caleb panted in between breaths, "now I see why Lucifer chose you." With those as his last words, Caleb closed his eyes.

Mazel dropped her swords and walked over to the other side of the room where she was chained to the wall. "We're going to chain him up because he's not dead. We don't have the dagger that'll kill him, but we have demon chains that'll weaken him." I nodded, too weak to say anything. I rolled on my stomach, grunting in pain as I slowly stood up.

"Raven, watch out!" Mazel yelled. I turned around just in time to see Caleb raise one of the swords high over his head.

Too weak to do anything, I closed my eyes as I waited for Caleb to strike me down. I heard him grunt and I opened my eyes. Protruding from the left side of his chest, was the Ambreison dagger. Caleb stared at me with wide eyes before he fell to the ground, dead. The room around me was spinning so fast.

I turned around, slowly and saw Lucifer, with his hair all wild and dark circles under his eyes. "Raven," Lucifer breathed, as he stared at me.

A small smile tugged at the corners of my lips. "Lucifer," I whispered as the world spun out of control and I passed out.

Officially Friends

When I became conscious again, I knew I was back home. Back in my bed that I shared with Lucifer, back in the safety of his fortified home, back in the place where I knew no harm could ever touch me again.

I smiled, my eyes closed. I wanted to move but I was too comfortable. I knew that I was injured but I didn't want to find out how injured I was.

I was about to go back to sleep when I heard someone open the door. I held really still.

"Sir, if I was you I would let her rest. She needs it desperately," a voice I identified as Leven advised. "She took a hell of a beating over at-" he stopped talking.

"I don't care what you think. You are not me. Now go away before I smite you," Lucifer growled. I heard Leven yelp and then his footsteps retreating.

I listened as Lucifer walked over to the bed. "Raven, I don't know if you can hear me but I am so sorry. I can't believe I let you out of my sight. If we had never had that fight, this never would have happened. I have never been so sorry in my entire existence. I am going to make it up to you, I promise," Lucifer swore.

"Apologizing is not a good color on you" I whispered, my voice hoarse. I opened my eyes and smiled when I saw Lucifer next to me. I sat up, with some effort. I noticed that I didn't have on my regular clothes. I ran my hands up and down my body and found I had a cloth around my breasts and my lower half. I had a bandage wrapped around my right shoulder and under my left rib cage. The biggest bandage was around my stomach. "You didn't um, change me, did you?"

"No, I didn't. Zaphara did that. Do you mind if I..." Lucifer trailed off. He seemed a bit uncomfortable.

"If you what?" I asked.

"If I hug you?" Lucifer whispered.

I sat there and stared at him. Was Lucifer asking to hug me? The King of the Underworld, the dude who gets anything he wants, was asking to hug me?

"Never mind," Lucifer said. "Forget I-"

"Yes," I nodded my head, smiling. "You can hug me. Let me get out of bed."

Lucifer waited until I was standing before he made his move. Very gently, he wrapped his arms around my waist. I smiled as I felt the warmth of his body against mine. This felt so right.

"I am so sorry," he kept saying over. He buried his head in my hair. "I honestly thought I had lost you. If you hadn't left me that clue, I never would have gotten there in time to save you."

"But, you did," I said, pulling him away from me. "You did save us just in time. If you hadn't of been there, Caleb would have killed me. As for Mazel..." I trailed off. "Wait! Mazel. Where is she?"

"She's fine," Lucifer tried to reassure me. "She is in her room recovering."

"I want to see her," I demanded. "She saved my life also. Without her, I never would have made it this far."

Lucifer looked like he was going to argue with me but decided against it. I guess he was afraid I might storm off again and get myself killed. "Let's go," he finally said.

I started to follow him out of the room when I realized I didn't have any clothes. "Um, Let me get dressed first."

Lucifer nodded and walked out of the room. After he shut the door, I went into the closet and found my outfit. It wasn't the most stylish but it was super comfortable: sweatpants and a baggy shirt.

I walked out of the room and told Lucifer to lead the way. Her bedroom was at the far end of the house. When we finally reached her door, Lucifer stood back. "Aren't you coming in with me?" I asked.

"Nope. She doesn't want to see me and something tells me it's best if you go in alone," Lucifer responded. "Besides, I have things I need to do."

Shrugging my shoulders a little bit, I went in and closed the door behind me. I scanned the room and found Mazel in the corner, sitting in front of a mirror.

"Mazel? Are you alright?" I quietly asked as I walked over to her.

Mazel looked at me with her eyes portraying how she felt: sad. "What's wrong sweetie?" I sat down next to her and pulled her into a hug.

"It's weird. You don't know how much you'll miss something until it's gone," she responded.

"You're wings?" I asked. She nodded. "If I could give them back to you, I would."

Mazel sighed, pushed me away, and stood up. "You can't give them back to me. God gave them to me."

"I know. I am so sorry. Hey, Maze...can I call you Maze?" I asked, reaching a hand out to her. She grabbed my hand and pulled me up.

Mazel shrugged and responded, "You just did."

Smiling, I continued. "I want to thank you for saving my life back when we were...you know. I honestly wouldn't have made it if it wasn't for you. I don't know exactly how things work down here but I owe you big time. If there is anything I could ever do for you, I will gladly do it."

"It was no big deal. I figured that if someone was worth saving, it was you. I may hate you but doesn't mean I want you dead."

Laughing, I gave Mazel a slight shove. "You don't hate me."

"You're right, I don't. You sort of saved my life too, Kitten. When I first met you, you were weak as fuck, or at least that is what I thought. Then, you took everything that Caleb threw your way and fought back. I have to say I was honestly impressed. My level of respect for you went way up."

I smiled at her, "Does this mean we are officially friends?"

Mazel frowned and thought for a minute. "Yeah, sure. We can be friends as long as there is no braiding hair or makeovers involved. Okay?"

Smiling, I nodded. Besides Michael, I don't think I have really ever had any other friend. Especially a friend who almost died with me. I guess that made us closer together than anything I have ever experienced with Michael.

Mazel's door swung open and in stepped Anthony. Anthony nodded at me looked over towards Mazel. They stood there for a minute, talking to each other, with their minds.

I slowly rocked back and forth on the balls of my feet while I waited for them to finish. It was sort of awkward between Anthony and me since I could not hear Anthony's mind speak. He couldn't actually speak because his tongue was cut by Zaphara. I was never told exactly why.

"Okay," Mazel clapped her hands together as Anthony walked out of the room, shutting the door behind her. "We have two hours to get ready."

"Ready for what, exactly?" I asked.

"From what I understood, Lucifer wants us all to have supper together. This, if I am being honest, is a first. Don't ask me what the occasion is because I honestly do not know."

"Okay," I said slowly. "So what do I need to do first?" I knew there was so much that needed to be done in order for me to look presentable for everyone. I just didn't know exactly where to start.

Mazel grabbed my arm and pulled me towards the bathroom "Well, considering the fact that we were held hostage by Caleb for about a week, I would probably start with a shower. Not to be rude, but when you walked into the room, I could smell you," she bluntly stated as she slammed the bathroom door in my face. From the other side of the door, she yelled, "You have thirty minutes to get a shower. So, I would suggest you get your stinky ass in that shower, now."

Will You Marry Me?

Two hours seemed to pass fairly quickly. I guess that is what happens when you are having fun. If that is what you can call getting ready for supper.

After I had finished showering, Mazel instructed me to dry my hair while she showered. Then when she finished, she helped me get ready while she got ready too. After we both got dressed, Mazel went to work on my appearance. Mazel plucked my eyes brows, she waxed my legs, she did my makeup, and she curled my hair.

"Okay," Mazel said, almost smiling, "you can now look." She spun me around and I gasped when I saw my reflection in the mirror.

If I am being completely honest, I have never considered myself to be a beautiful person. Yeah, I am not ugly, but beautiful would be crossing the line. I was never one to wear makeup because I was never taught how to apply makeup.

Mazel had done a wonderful job on my face. I actually felt really pretty, for the first time in my life. Mazel actually did a good job on my makeup, I thought to myself. Then I burst out laughing.

"What is so funny?" Mazel asked as she put the final touches on her face.

"Earlier you said that we could be friends as long as no makeovers are involved," I smiled.

"Do not get used to it," Mazel replied. "This is a one-time deal."

At that moment, Mazel's door flew open and Anthony and Leven walked into the room. They were both dressed up in fancy suits. Leven's suit was a light blue color with a black rose pinned to the collar. He looked really cute for a fifteen-year-old. Anthony's suit was a deep purple color with a white color. He also had a black rose pinned to the collar.

"Wow," I smiled, "You both look great."

Leven stepped towards me and held out his arm. "Miss Hunter, I will be your escort to the dining room, tonight."

Laughing, I took his arm. I looked over at Mazel who took Anthony's arm. Whatever was going on didn't bother me one bit. Yes, it was a complete change from before I was kidnapped, but I am not even going to complain about it.

When we reached the dining room, I gasped. It was different from the last time I saw it, over a week ago. The wall color used to be black but now it was light red and purple. Candles were on all the shelves that lined the walls. The table was lined with all kinds of food. It all looked and smelt so amazing. Wine glasses were in front of every chair. Classical music was playing somewhere in the room, at a quieter volume. The room was so much more inviting than the last time I remembered it.

Leven led me to my spot, next to the captain chair, and then walked to the other side of the table. Mazel stood next to me. Leven and Anthony walked to the other side of the table and stood behind their chairs.

I was about to sit down when Mazel grabbed my arm and shook her head. The door to the ballroom opened up and Miss Lillie and Zaphara walked into the room, arm-in-arm. They went to a spot at the table and stood behind their chairs.

We stood behind our chairs for a few minutes when I started to get impatient. I was tired of standing and I was so hungry. I can't even remember the last time I ate. I started to ask where Lucifer was when he walked into the room.

My heart started to skip a couple of beats when he walked over to the table, never breaking eye contact with me. He looked so much better than when I saw him two hours ago. His face actually had color to it and he finally brushed his hair. The dark circles under his eyes were gone and his eyes had a sparkle to them. He wasn't dressed up as fancy as Leven and Anthony, but he didn't need to. He looked so handsome the way he was.

"Miss Hunter," Lucifer nodded at me, as he pulled my chair out.

"Mr. DeVil," I smiled as I sat down in my chair and he pushed it up to the table. Lucifer walked to his seat and once he sat down, everyone else did the same.

"So," I started, waving my hands around the room. "What is this all about? Why is everyone here?"

"Before we get to that, I want to say a few things." Lucifer grabbed the glass in front of him, which was filled with wine and raised it into the air. "I want to say that I am so glad that Raven and Mazel is back home safe. I was tearing through Hell trying to find you both."

Mazel scoffed and I glared at her. I was going to say something, but Lucifer continued. "I'm being serious Mazel. When I couldn't find either you or Raven, I knew you had both been taken. When I found out that my best friend was gone too, I knew exactly what had happened. I just didn't know where he was. I thank Raven for the clue. You were so brilliant, Angel." I shot him a glare because he knew I didn't like his nickname for me. "I also knew that as long as Raven was with you, Mazel, no matter how much you hate her, you would try your best to protect her. For that, I am so grateful. I don't know what I would do if Raven..." He didn't finish his sentence. We all knew what he was going to say.

Clearing his throat he continued, "Anyway, a toast to safe returns and new beginnings."

Everyone raised their glass and drank to that. I sat there, staring at my glass. I knew it was filled with wine and I wasn't old enough to drink yet. Lucifer seemed to notice and asked me why I wasn't drinking to his toast.

"Wow, this is sort of embarrassing, but I am not old enough to drink."

Everyone around me started laughing and I felt my cheeks heat up. "Raven," Lucifer said between breaths, "you are in Hell. Anything goes here. There are no rules here unless I say. But I understand you still holding on to the human rules so here," Lucifer touched my glass and the liquid in the glass turned to water.

Smiling, I lifted the glass to my lips and took a tiny sip. "Thank you," I said after I finished the water. When I set the glass down on the table, it instantly filled up with water. "Wow."

"Now, I know you all want to eat but I have one other thing I want to say." Lucifer scooted his chair out from the table and held out his hand. I cautiously put my hand in his.

"Raven, I have a confession to make. When you was gone, I was so lost without you. I didn't even eat the entire time you were gone. I didn't do anything but spend all my time looking for you. I will admit that when I marked you eleven years ago, it was for my own selfish reasons. I knew you were special and I wanted to use you for my own gain."

Surprised, I pulled my hand back. "You were going to use me?"

"Yes," Lucifer nodded, "but all my plans melted away when I met you for the first time at the high school. I knew at that moment, you were not the same little girl I met that day at the park. I want you to know now, that I want to do nothing but protect you for the rest of your life.

"When I finally got you back, I realized something: I don't think I-No, I know I can't live my life without you. Raven, seeing you on that floor, unconscious, made me realize that I broke a promise. I made a promise to your parents the day they died that I would protect you for as long as you live. I broke that promise and I am truly sorry.

"Remember when I told you that love could not exist in this place?" I nodded. How could I forget? "Well, I lied."

Lucifer got out of his chair. He reached behind him and pulled out a small red and black box. Everyone in the room gasped. "Lucifer. What are you doing?" I whispered. My heart was beating so fast I thought I was going to throw up.

Lucifer grabbed my hand and got down on one knee. He opened the box and inside of it was a beautiful ring. It had skulls around the black band. In the middle, rested a huge red ruby and on either side of that ruby were wings. "Charity Raven Hunter, will you marry me?"

Goodnight

I looked around the room as everyone was staring at me. I caught Mazel's eyes and raised an eyebrow. She gave me a slight nod and I smiled. "Yes," I cried. "I will marry you."

Lucifer slipped the ring on my finger and stood up. "Raven, I love you so much. I really do." He picked me up and spun me around.

I grimaced and he quickly set me down. "Did I hurt you? I am so sorry."

"You're fine. It's just my wounds need to heal a bit more before we do any twirling," I smiled at him.

"I hope you all enjoy your meal," Lucifer said as I sat in my chair. He pushed me up to the table again and then he sat down.

Instantly, everyone started filling their plates up. I sat there, examining the ring. It honestly was beautiful. Never, in a million years did I ever think I was going to get married let alone to a guy I didn't even believe existed until a month ago.

"So, when exactly are you and the Kitten going to get married?" Mazel asked Lucifer.

"Oh my, I haven't even thought of that." Lucifer put his fork down and looked at me. "Any suggestions?" I shook my head. "Well, if it was up to me, I would get married tonight."

"Nu-uh," Mazel said. "You are not getting married tonight. You need time to figure out where you're going to get married at. She needs times to get herself a dress. The setting has to be right. You need to figure out a guest list, invitations need to be sent. Hey, you were going to have a ball before the whole kidnapping happened. Why don't you use that as a platform to get the word out?" Mazel suggested. "Then by the end of the week, you both can get married if you'd like."

Lucifer looked at me and asked, "What do you think, Rave? Do you want to do the ball thing still?"

"No one is going to eat me while I'm there, are they?" I didn't mean it as a joke but that is how everyone took it.

"As long as you're with me, you should be fine, Angel. Let's eat and then we can start making plans after supper."

After supper, I went to my room and Lucifer followed right behind me. "Are you okay, Angel?"

"Yeah, I am. I am just tired." I walked into the closet and changed into my night clothes. When I finished I walked out and continued as I made my way to the bed. "Everything is happening so fast. Just a month ago, I met you and now I am getting smarried. This stuff only ever happens in fairytales." I pulled down the covers and crawled in bed.

"The rest of our lives can be a fairy tale if you want. We are both immortal so we will live forever." Lucifer got into bed, laying on top of the covers.

He laid on his side and faced me. "I want to kiss you so bad but I want to wait until we get married."

"But we have already kissed once," I told him. "Remember the day when I threw myself off the building?"

"Yeah, I remember. What a stupid thing to do, by the way. You could have been killed. But that was before I knew that I loved you."

"So, when exactly, did you figure it out?" I asked, yawning.

"Seconds after the first kiss," Lucifer responded.

"That-That doesn't make any sense."

"Yes, it does. I asked you to kiss me because I wanted to see what it was like to kiss something as pure as you. I know that sounds selfish but-"

"A lot of things you have done with me have been selfish," I sighed.

"But," Lucifer tired again, "after you broke away from that kiss, I wanted more. I had never felt like that with anyone before. I never wanted it to end and I knew at that moment that I truly loved you. How about you? When did you know that you truly loved me?"

"Oh. I think it was when you saved me from that guy almost killing me. You know the day I woke up this bed? I don't know but something about someone risking it all to save me is something I have always wanted. I have a great deal of time by myself with no one to care for me but Michael. I just wanted someone to care if I happened to disappear one day."

"Well, I will always care for you no matter what. I want to spend the rest of my life with you and maybe even have a family together. I have always wanted kids but I don't know really how that would work. You know, with me being all dead?"

"Um...yeah. Let's just take one day at a time, Luci." I yawned again and smiled. "I'm going to sleep. Goodnight."

Lucifer said goodnight and turned on his left side, facing the bathroom. Within minutes, he was asleep.

Poor thing, he probably hasn't even slept since I have been gone. I wish I could fall asleep that fast.

Everything that happened in the last few days started to swirl around in my mind. I would never have imagined encountering any of this. It is just crazy to even think about it.

Since I wasn't that sleepy, I got up and walked to the bathroom. I quietly shut the door and locked it. I did not want Lucifer to walk on me.

Very carefully, I took off my clothes. I wanted to see my wounds. I first took the bandage off my shoulder. But, how? It was just a day ago when I got this? The wound was almost gone. A long, jagged scar was in its place. Quickly, I tore off the bandage from around my rib and my stomach. They were both the same way. A scar was in the place of the wound.

Maybe healing really fast is one of my special abilities. I thought to myself, yawning once again.

Putting my clothes back on, I unlocked the door and headed to bed. I was too tired to do any more thinking.

I crawled back under the covers and tried my best to fall asleep. Lucifer turned from his left to his right side. His eyes were closed and his breathing was still of that of someone sleeping. He was so handsome. I am so lucky to be marrying someone like him.

I took one more look at his face and closed my eyes. I could have sworn I heard someone whisper, "Please don't ever leave me," before I fell asleep.

Nightmare

I waited until the music started playing before I entered the room. Once the music started, the doors opened for me. I slowly walked into the room, smiling. I have been waiting for this day for so long and it is now here.

Everyone around me stared at me as I walked down the aisle. I could barely contain my excitement.

Before I stepped up to the altar, I took a deep breath. From this moment on, my life was going to be completely different.

A guy, who is I is the minister, stood in front of me, not smiling. That's weird, I thought to myself. Why isn't he smiling?

I spun around and noticed that no one in the audience was smiling either. "What's going on?" I asked, aloud. Something about this entire thing seemed off. Weddings should be a happy place. People should be smiling and crying. The groom should be up on the alter looking nervous. The groom, I thought to myself as I looked around the room. "Where is Lucifer?"

"I'm right here," Lucifer said as he walked into the room. His hair was a mess and dark circles rested under his eyes. He was dressed up in a black suit but his suit was ripped up.

"Wha-What happened to you?"

"Don't worry about it, babe. Let's just get this over with. I have more important things to attend to." Lucifer smiled.

I took a step back, shocked. "What's more important than marrying me?"

"You'll see," Lucifer winked at me and motioned for the minister to start.

Uneasy, I turned to the minister and listened to him ramble on about love and how it is a powerful thing. How we truly are one of a kind and a perfect match made in heaven.

The minister turned to me and spoke, "Raven Charity Hunter, do you-"

"It's Charity Raven Hunter," I corrected him.

The minister stood there, glaring at me. "Don't speak unless spoken to, little girl."

My mouth fell open from his response. I wanted to say something but I decided against it.

The minister, after staring at me a few seconds longer, continued. "Charity Raven Hunter," he spat. "Do you take Lucifer, King of Underworld, ruler of all that is evil, God's first Angel, as your husband?"

A smile crept up on my face, as I turned to look at Lucifer. Even in his tired looking state, he was still the most beautiful person I have ever seen. "I do."

"Lucifer, do you take Charity Raven Hunter to be your wife?"

Lucifer turned to me and nodded. "I do."

"Then by the power invested in me, I now pronounce you husband and wife." He looked at Lucifer and said, "You may now kiss your bride."

Lucifer smiled and leaned in to kiss me. The kiss wasn't as magical as the first time we kissed but it was still nice. When we pulled away, I whispered in his ear, "How about we get out of here and you show me what is so important?"

Lucifer told me to turn around so that my back was facing him. Smiling, I turned my back and waited. Around me, people started to whisper something, together but I couldn't make out what they were saying. The whispers gradually got louder and I could make out what they were saying.

"Sacrifice, Sacrifice, Sacrifice!" They all chanted.

"Sacrifice?" I repeated, confused. "Lucifer, what are they talking about?" I asked. I heard what sounded like a blade unsheathing and I quickly spun around. I screamed as Lucifer thrust the sword in my stomach.

"Why?" I cried, as he pulled the blade out. Red started to spread everywhere on my white gown. Shocked, I grabbed my stomach and fell to my knees.

"I was going to stab you in the back but you turned around too quickly, darling. It doesn't matter, though. I have been after your soul since the day your parents cut a deal with me. Now, I will finally have it and there is nothing you can do about it!"

Lucifer smiled as he raised the sword above his left shoulder. "Your time has finally come." He let out a yell, down came to the sword, and-

I screamed as I sat up in the bed. Thankful that it was nothing but a nightmare, I cried.

Lucifer instantly sat up and turned on the lamplight. "Raven, what's wrong?" He reached out to touch my shoulder and I jerked away from him.

"Don't-Don't touch me," I cried.

"What happened?" He asked as he jerked his hand back, quickly.

"You-my dream. We were at the altar. We had just said our vows. You t-told me to t-turn away from you. The audience was chanting 'sacrifice'. I heard a noise be-behind me and as I turned to face you, y-you stabbed me. You were going to stab me in the back but I caught you. And then you were going to cut off my h-head."

"Oh, Rave, that was nothing but a nightmare. I would never stab you in the back. If I was going to kill anyone, I would want to see the defeat in their eyes."

"You're not helping me!" I yelled.

"Raven, darling, it was but a dream. You are under so much pressure. With the horrible week you have had, I would be so surprised if you didn't have these kind of dreams."

"What if it's Caleb sending me a message? He did say when he branded me," I pulled up the sleeve to my top to reveal my shoulder, "that I would never be rid of him."

Lucifer laughed at me, which caused me to glare at him. "Angel, there is a reason why I keep the Ambreison Dagger down in the basement. When you stabbed an immortal with the Dagger, especially in the heart, their soul is instantly destroyed. Yes, Caleb was a demon but he was once an Angel first. When I was no longer welcomed in Heaven, Caleb decided to follow me to Hell. So, believe me when I tell you, there is no way in Hell that Caleb is still alive. In addition, we threw his body into the burning pits. It's safe to say, he is officially gone."

"But what about the-"

"The brand? Yes, it will be with you forever. However, do not let the memory of the person, who gave you that brand, bring you down. Instead, use that brand as a symbol of strength. Use it as a reminder of everything you've endured and how it has made you a stronger person. Let it give you the strength to overcome anything else life throws your way."

Nodding my head, I sighed. "I guess I am just stressed over everything I have been through. I just need some rest."

"That's right. You just need some rest. Get some sleep. We have a big day tomorrow and I need you rested. Goodnight, Raven." Lucifer smiled at me and then laid back down on the bed. Within seconds, he was fast asleep.

Shaking my head, I laid back down and watched him sleep. I don't know exactly when I, too, fell asleep but I did and I had no more bad dreams for the rest of the night.

Wedding Plans

"Raven are you sure this is what you want to do on our wedding?" Lucifer asked, frowning slightly. "It's in two days so we do not have any room for errors."

I nodded my head and smiled. "Yes, I think it will be super romantic. Besides, weddings are supposed to take place in a peaceful environment. No offense, but your idea of having our wedding here sort of defeats the purpose of peaceful."

Lucifer raised an eyebrow. "You don't think having our wedding with all the tortured souls screaming around us is romantic?"

Rolling my eyes, I smacked his arm. "Be serious. I want this wedding to be perfect. I am only planning on getting married once to the man I want to spend the rest of my life with."

Lucifer smiled. "I am the luckiest guy alive...or rather dead. I don't really know where I would stand at this point."

Shaking my head, I said, "It doesn't really matter to me. If you meet me at the altar on our wedding day, I won't argue with you. Now," I stood up from the table, "if you will excuse me, I need to compile a list of people we are going to invite. I'll see you later."

"I am almost done setting up for the ball. The invitations went out last week, but I had postponed it because-" He couldn't bring himself to finish his sentence.

"Luci, it's fine. I know what you mean. I still need to find a dress for the ball, but I'll do that later today."

"Raven, you know the ball is-"

"Tomorrow, yes, I know. Lucifer, you need to take a deep breath and relax. You got this." I patted his arm. It seems, lately, all he ever does is worry.

"I know. I just want this to be perfect. You go and do your thing and I'll see you tonight."

Smiling, I left the room before he could think of anything else to talk about.

"I don't know why he is so tense, Zap. I know even since I have been gone he's been working like a madman to find me. But I'm here now and he is still so tense."

Zaphara walked out of her closet with an armful of dresses. "Darling, you just need to calm down. He is always like this. Now, what do you think about these dresses?"

Sighing, I stood up from the bed. After I had made the list of people I was going to invite, I went to Zaphara for help on finding a dress.

Since the ball is tomorrow we did not have time to get a new dress made. As for my wedding dress, Miss Lillie has been working on it nonstop since

I have returned, three days ago. My wedding day will be on Sunday. Kind of ironic, right?

"Remind me again," I started as I went through the handful of dresses on Zaphara's bed, "why I have to go to this ball."

"Think of it like a Coronation, except for the fact that you are not being crowned queen. This ball will have the most powerful rulers from all Nine Realms present. This is the only way Lucifer can introduce you to everyone while conducting his yearly business meeting."

I put down the blue dress I had been inspecting, on the bed. "His...his business meeting?" I didn't see anything while I looked through the stack, so I went into her closet and searched for a dress.

"Yeah, each year Lucifer and the rulers of the Nine meet to go over any new news. Hell is its own world and like Earth, there are rulers of certain territory. Now Lucifer is the ruler of them all. The Nine may be presidents but Lucifer is the King. Does that make sense?"

I stuck my head out of the closet, nodded, and then smiled. I found the perfect dress. "This is the one, Z. I want to wear this one."

Walking out of the closet, I presented the dress I had tried on. The top of the dress was black. Elastic ran around the waist, which is where the black ended. Pink, purple, and coral colors exploded in a messy assortment below the elastic line. They started out dark and the closer they got to the bottom of the dress, the lighter the colors got until they went completely white. The best part of the dress was the fact it was strapless.

"Really?" Zaphara grimaced at the dress. "That is what you want to wear tomorrow?"

"Yes," I said, laughing. "What is wrong with it?"

"Nothing, I guess. I don't remember buying that dress. It must be Lillith's dress."

"No matter who it belongs to, I want to wear this dress tomorrow."

Slowly nodding her head, Zaphara agreed. She grabbed her cushion of pins and beckoned me over to the block in the center of the room. "Then this dress will be the one. Get up on the block so I can see what needs to be taken in before tomorrow." Once I was up on the block, Zaphara went to work. "So tell me Raven, what did you plan for the big day?"

Smiling, I told Zaphara everything. The wedding would take place on Earth, under the oldest tree in the town I grew up in. I was told, when my parents were still alive, this is where they got married. The handful of people I invited to the wedding would be there, hopefully, with smiling faces. I want the wedding to take place at sunset. I have always thought that was the most romantic time of the day.

I want Mazel to be my maid of honor because of everything we have been through, I feel like we share a special kind of bond. Since my parents aren't alive neither one of them can give me away. I have decided that I want the person who has been in my life the most, to give me away. I sent out a text to Micheal but sadly, he hasn't responded back. I don't know if anyone will be giving me away. I asked Miss Lillie to officiate the wedding, which she said she would, happily.

The vows would be next, which I finished last night. It is nothing extravagant, but I wouldn't change anything on it. I know Lucifer is still working on his, but he promised me it would be done in time. The entire thing is simple but I believe it's going to be absolutely perfect.

"I don't know, Zap, do you think this is going to be enough? I know it is very simple, but I want a simple yet unforgettable wedding."

"Raven," Zaphara looked up at me, putting the last pin in my gown. "this is your wedding. You do whatever you think is going to be right. Does this feel right?"

I nodded and smiled. It honestly did feel right. For the first time in my life I actually feel like I have a purpose.

"Well, there you go. I know Luci is super excited. My brother is finally getting married and will finally be happy for the first time in his life. Now, go take off this dress, carefully."

I stepped down off the block and went into the closet. I couldn't wait for the newest chapter of my life to begin.

Not Invited

The next day was absolutely busy. Everyone in the house kept rushing past me, barely stopping to talk.

"Hey, what's on the menu for tonight?" I asked one of the maids, that I have seen around the house the few times I have gone to the kitchen.

"Sorry Mistress Hunter, I have no time to talk," the lady said to me as she grabbed a tray full of fruit from the chef.

"But-" The lady disappeared behind a door, not before she shot me a look of jealously? Not really sure why she would be jealous of me.

After trying to talk to several different people, and getting multiple of nasty looks in return, I gave up.

I have always loved the sound of nature, but you know, being where I currently am and all, I couldn't really enjoy those sounds. I mean I could be sadistic and enjoy the sounds of tortured souls receiving forever and a year of punishment, but that really isn't my cup of tea.

I left the first floor of the house and went up to the second floor, to my room. When I opened the door, I found Anthony sitting on the foot of the bed.

"Um, hello. What are you doing in my room?" I asked him. He stood up and stared at me.

After a few seconds of awkward silence, I gave up. I couldn't hear anything Anthony was saying. For some odd reason, I lack that ability.

"It's fine. Don't tell me." I walked over to my bed and flopped down on the mattress. "Is it always this hectic when Lucifer holds a ball?" I asked.

Anthony shook his head and continued to stare at me.

"I do not know why someone would hold a ball at midnight. On top of that, it's going to last four hours! Come on! Now, if you are not here for any specific reason, I would like you to get out of my room. The ball starts in three hours and I would like to get some sleep."

Anthony shook his head again and motioned for me to follow him. "Come on!" I complained. "I just laid down." I got up from the bed and followed Anthony.

I followed Anthony to the basement of the house. "You know, being down here brings back memories," I shuddered. Last time I was down here, bad things happened.

Anthony gave me an apologetic look and continued walking. Finally, he stopped in front of the room that Miss Lillie and Zaphara shared. "Oh, you could have told me this is where I was going," I said. "Well, I guess you would have if I could hear you. Thanks, big guy, I'll see you later? You're going to be at the ball, right?"

Anthony shook his head. "But why?" I asked him. He once again stared at me, and I sighed. "You know what, do you know sign language?"

He nodded his head. "Really? Wow, I wish I knew that a long time ago."

"Okay, so tell me, why won't you be at the ball?"

After thinking for a second, he finally started to sign. Not invited.

"What? You weren't invited? Why?"

Because no one asked me to go. It is an exclusive ball. Important people only get in.

"But, you are important," I said.

Anthony shook his head. Not really.

"You are important, Anthony, and I want you to come. Okay? I am inviting you to this ball."

Anthony nodded his head slightly and looked behind me. I turned around to see Zaphara and Miss Lillie standing there.

"You can't just invite anyone," Miss Lillie said. "He doesn't hold any kind of status down here."

"I don't understand why not."

"See, besides the Nine being at the party later today, I will be there because I am one of the original fates. Zaphara will be there because she is Lucifer's sister. Mazel will be there because she is Mazel and she is one of the very first angel turned demon. Leven will be there because he is Lucifer's servant. And you will be there because you will soon be Lucifer's wife, making you the Queen of the Underworld."

"Well, like you said, I will soon be a ruler of Hell. That means my word is just as important." I turned and faced Anthony. "You will come to the ball. You are invited and anyone who says otherwise can come and speak to me."

Anthony bowed his head and smiled slightly. He then walked away. I really hope I didn't just make a mistake, I thought to myself.

I turned back around and faced Miss Lillie and Zaphara. They were both smiling. "What?" I asked.

"Look at you," Zaphara smiled. "You aren't even married, and you are already bossing guys around."

"Well, I want everyone I like to be there. Besides, I do not do well with others telling me what I can and cannot do. Speaking of which, what am I doing down here?"

"Ah," Miss Lillie held up a finger. "Follow us. We were told to get you ready for the ball. In less than three hours it will start, and we need to make you presentable."

"It takes three hours to make me look presentable?" I asked.

"No," Zaphara said, rolling her eyes. "But it does take about two hours to tell you how to act at a ball, what you can an cannot eat, and to educate you on all of the Nine."

"What happens if I don't want to learn all that stuff?"

Miss Lillie and Zaphara looked at each other and then looked at me. "Oh, Girl," Zaphara spoke, "you don't even want to think about that. In case you haven't noticed, you're in Hell. Everything and everyone, besides the people you trust in this house, is trying to kill you. If you do the wrong thing at the ball, you could die. If you eat the wrong thing, you will die. If you say the wrong thing to the wrong person, you-"

"Let me guess," I interrupted. "I could die?"

"Yes," Zaphara nodded. "A very painful and horrible death. The people at this ball are the worst of the worst. There is a reason Lucifer chose them to take over a certain part of the Realm. I remember the last ball that was held, over a few thousand years ago, a servant accidently bumped into one of the Nine. Let's just say that he can no longer walk, talk, or see. And he got off easy.

So, tonight, you are walking across a tightrope. One wrong step and you fall to your death. Do you understand?"

Both Zaphara and Miss Lillie gave me serious look. This night was supposed to be a fun night but turns out there is a huge chance I might die. Feeling all the color rush from my face I whispered, "Got it."

(1154 words)

Started: 9-7-18

Ended: 9-9-18

Updated: 9-12-18

Entertainment

I spent the first hour getting ready for the ball. I showered, shaved, and dried my hair and put on my dress. Miss Lillie worked on my hair while Zaphara did my make-up. After they were finished, they went to work on educating me on how to stay alive for tonight. We've been at it for two hours and forty-six minutes.

"Okay, we have about ten minutes left. Let's go over this one more time. If Mikel Razoul ever approaches you, what do you do?"

"Um, I am to never accept any offer he throws my way."

"Why?" Miss Lillie asked.

"Because he rules the greed realm," I said, bored. "Can we just please stop? I am bored, and I need a break."

Miss Lillie and Zaphara looked at each other. Zaphara shrugged which cause Miss Lillie to sigh. "Fine, Raven," Miss Lillie said. "But for everyone's sake, if you don't remember what to do, do not say anything. The worse you can do there is offend them with your silence."

"Okay, fine, whatever," I replied. "Can I go now?"

Miss Lillie shook her head and walked over to the door. "It is time to head to the ballroom anyway. Don't show them any fear and have fun."

I nodded and took off out the door. I ran down the stairs, careful not to break trip in my heels. Who knew that growing up was so hard?

When I reached the bottom of the stairs, I straightened up my dress and my hair. I quickly, but quietly walked to the ball room. This night was one of the biggest nights of my life and if I don't play my cards right, it might be the last.

Finally, after going through three more rooms, I reached the ballroom. The door was shut and one of the servants stood at the door. Seeing me, he gave me a slight nod and opened the door for me.

As soon as the door opened, it was like a sensory overload. Classical music was blaring through the speakers, hundreds of people were in the room, the lights were changing colors, and the aroma from all the food, were flooding my senses.

"So, this is what a part looks like," I said to myself. Taking a deep breath, I walked into the room. I quietly, walked around the room, looking for the one person I loved. After surveying the room for about ten minutes, I gave up. He wasn't here yet.

Over on the far-right wall were the tables. As I made my way over to them, someone grabbed my arm. I spun around to face the person.

The person was a guy who looked to be in his late forties. He had greasy brown hair with red streaks running through them. Running from the left side of his face, starting above his eyebrow, to the bottom right, below his jaw, was a jagged scar. His left eye was sewn shut and his right eye was completely black.

"Where do you think you're going, pretty lady?" the guy asked me.

I tried to jerk away from him, but he held firmly to my arm. "I-I," I started but then stop. Show no fear, Raven. "I'm going to go sit down at a table. Now, I think it would benefit you to release me."

The guy stood there and laughed, "Benefit me? Who do you think you are?"

"Raven!" a voice called from across the room. "There you are."

The crowd parted as Mazel made her way over to me and the guy. The entire room went quiet as they watched her walk over to us.

When Mazel stopped in front of us, she gave the guy a slight nod. "Nigel didn't know you were going to be here."

Nigel smirked and replied, "You don't know much, do you? Maybe if you spent less time in the bedrooms and more time being useful you would know. You whore!"

Everyone gasped as Mazel growled at Nigel. I was not going to stand this!

Without even thinking, I stomped on Nigel's foot, as hard as I could in heels. "That was for touching me!"

Once he released me, I punched him in the face. "And that was for calling my best friend a whore, you bastard."

Blood started to flow from Nigel's nose. "Why you little b-"

"Is there a problem here?" a voice, I knew all too well, asked.

Standing in the door way of the ballroom was Lucifer and nine other people. One would have to be a dummy to not know who they were. As soon as they stepped into the room, the air changed. A sense of power seemed to feel the air as all nine people entered the room.

Instantly my face lit up as he and the Nine walked over to us. Around the room, people started to whisper. It is not very often one witnesses all nine rulers and Lucifer together in one room.

When Lucifer reached us, he opened his arms for an embrace. "Raven, darling, how is my fiancée?"

Smiling, I hugged Lucifer. He smelt so amazing. I never wanted to let go of him. "Well, truthfully? It was going amazing until Nigel, here, grabbed my arm. He then called Mazel a whore."

"Oh?" Lucifer cocked his head to the side and looked at Nigel. "So, what she is telling me is that you touched her without her permission?"

"Well, um, in my um defense, I didn't know that she was your um, fiancée. I thought she was one of your slaves. I am so terribly sorry," Nigel apologized, profusely, even though, I could see it in his eyes, he knew it wasn't going to be enough.

Lucifer shook his head, smiling. "Sorry? I am so sick and tired of hearing that word here. Sorry doesn't get you to heaven and in your case, sorry won't save your pathetic ass."

Lucifer turned to the Nine and asked, "How long has it been since you all have had fun at my party?"

"Let'sss ssseee," spoke the only female in the group. "It's been a few thousand yearsss ssince we have had fun."

"That has been a while," Lucifer said, as he shoved Nigel towards the Nine. "He's all yours. Have fun."

Lucifer held his hand out for me, and I took it. He led me away from the Nine. "What are they going to do to him?" I asked, as they circled him.

"Whatever they want to," Lucifer responded, as we approached the front of the room. "I never really did like him anyway. I've been trying to get rid of him for a while now."

I heard Nigel scream, and I quickly turn around. The female let out a screech as she pounced on him. The other piled on top. Lucifer gently touched my face and turned it in his direction. "Don't worry about them, they love putting on a show."

After a few minutes, Nigel's screams were silent. Two people from the crowd grabbed his arounds and pulled him through the crowd. I gasped when I saw him. Blood was dripping from his mouth, staining his white suit. His other eye was gouged out, leaving a hole of nothingness. All of his fingers were missing. All of them. They had pulled all his fingers off.

"Oh my-" I gasped. "Why would they do such a thing?" I asked as the Nine walked to the front of the room.

Lucifer smiled. "Angel, Nigel got off easy," he responded as him and the two people helping him, passed us.

Once they had left the room, everyone looked at Lucifer and the Nine. They had taken their spot on the stage, next to us.

"Okay, now that we have had our entertainment for the night, how about we get this party started?"

(1310 words)

A King's Meal

For the rest of the night, we had fun. Lucifer and I danced to seventeen songs. Even though, I know most, if not all, of the Nine wanted to dance with me.

Lucifer must have known that being around them made me nervous, so he made sure he was next to my side the rest of the night.

After seeing what they did to Nigel, I was terrified for my life, even though I knew that Lucifer would never let them rip me apart.

After Lucifer and I were done dancing, we both sat in our chairs. Even though Lucifer doesn't call them thrones, they are. They are both stationed on a higher floor than the rest of the room. His chair was made from a very interesting material. The seat, the arm rest, and the back rest was comprised of human, and I'm pretty sure, demon bones. Strips of gold spiraled around the arms rests, the back rest and even the seats of the chair. This gave the chair a look of importance. Even though, I know I should have been disgusted, I wasn't. The chair, in its own unique way, was very beautiful.

My chair was like his, but only smaller. Instead of having gold wrapped around the arm, the back and the seat of the chair, silver stood in its place. I guess we all can figure out which chair belonged to who.

"Sorry about the color," Lucifer said. "Before you came along, that seat belonged to Zaphara. I know it sounds like you are getting her hand-me-downs, but she actually wanted you to have it. If you want to, we can change the color to gold."

I smiled, he was too sweet. "I like it just the way it is."

"Good," he said, smiling.

We sat in our chairs and watched everyone dance around. It seemed like most of the people here, were drunk.

After what seemed like hours, the party calmed down. All of the people, minus the helpers and the Nine were on the ground, asleep. "What time is it?" I asked Lucifer.

"It is exactly four o'clock," he responded.

Mikel Razoul, approached us after the last person fell to the ground. "Lucifer, it has been hours since we have eaten. We were wondering what you had in store for us?"

"Well, I'm guessing you all don't want the food that my staff has prepared for you, do you?" Lucifer asked, even though he and I both knew the answer.

"Come on, Luci, you know us better than that."

Lucifer smiled. "I do. Why do you think I invited so many humans to the ball? It certainly wasn't to eat up all the food. There is enough people here for you all to have a king's meal."

Mikel's eyes changed from blue to black as he smiled. "Thanks buddy," he said, as he left us alone.

Mikel walked back to the group and told him of what Lucifer said. I could see them all picking out which group of people they were going to indulge on. I shivered at the thought of being their next meal.

"Now, for my beautiful wife to be, we will be dining in the Great Hall." Lucifer stood up and offered me a hand. Smiling, I took it.

Mikel followed behind us, as we walked towards the doors. Once we were out of the room, he smirked at me, and locked the doors behind him.

Once again, I shivered. As we went to the Great Hall, we could hear the screams of the Nine's terrified victims.

Lucifer smiled as entered the Hall. The table was filled with food. From roasted chicken, to pizza, to all kinds of soups and vegetables and even fruits.

He pulled out my chair and I sat down. Once I was seated, he pushed my chair in. He then sat down and laughed.

"What's so funny?" I asked, smiling. I wanted to be part of his joke.

"Never trust a demon," Lucifer said, still laughing. My smiled instantly disappeared. "I knew that you would not eat what was set out at the table in the ballroom, so I told the staff to make American food. I hope you like pizza, chicken and everything else on this table."

"I do," I said, slightly smiling.

"Then dig in! I especially love pizza!" he said, as he grabbed five slices.

"Um, you sure it is safe? I mean you did just say to 'never trust a demon'?"

"Raven, you should know by now I would never intentionally hurt you. I love you more than I have ever loved anything. Do you think I would poison your food?"

"No," I whispered, as I grabbed a slice of pizza and a spoonful of vegetables. "I'm just worried that one of these days I'm going to wake up and find it all to be a dream."

"Raven, this is not a dream. This is real life, trust me. This is my life and your life. This life right here, is our life. In less than fifteen hours, you and I will be married, and I will never want for another thing again."

I smiled, tears in my eyes, and grabbed Lucifer hand. I gave his hand a tight squeeze. "Thank you so much." I said.

"You're welcome, my Angel. Now, I don't know about you, but I am absolutely famished."

Lucifer and I ate as much as we could. I was so full that if I ate anything else, I would through up.

"Why did we do that?" he asked me, as we walked into our bedroom. He shut the door and instantly started taking off his suit.

"I don't know," I replied. "But with a little bit of sleep, we should be fine before our wedding." I walked into the closet and changed out of my clothes. I then walked to the bathroom and removed all the makeup from my face.

Wedding. I am getting married in less than fourteen hours. I walked out of the closet smiling. I found Lucifer laying on the bed, above the covers.

Ever since my first day in Hell, he has slept on top of the covers. He didn't want me to worry about him taking my innocence, even though, he knew I knew he wouldn't.

"Why are you smiling, my Angel?" he asked, motioning for me to get in to bed.

"Wedding. I am getting married in less than fourteen hours. Can you believe it?"

"I am the one who can't believe it. I have been waiting for this day for you don't even know how long. And on top of that, I hit the jackpot with you. You are everything I wanted and more."

I could feel my cheeks heat up. Was I blushing? I don't blush...do I?

"Tomorrow is going to be the best day of my life," I said, as I hugged Lucifer goodnight.

"Correction," he said. "Our life."

(1160 words)

Started: 9-13-18

Ended: 9-13-18

His Diabolic Angel

"Raven are you ready?" Zaphara called from outside my bedroom.

"Give me one more minute!" I called. I was trying to put on my left shoes. I didn't want to wrinkle my dress by sitting down on the bed, so I have been trying to put my shoe on standing up.

"Raven, we need time to get to the wedding. Lucifer is waiting for you at the altar. If I have to listen to him ask me if you still want to get married, I might take the Dagger and kill him."

I rolled my eyes, as I finally got my shoe on and strapped. I opened the door, slightly to find Zaphara leaning against the hallway wall, talking on her phone.

"As soon as she gets her shoes on, we will be going," she said into the phone. "No, I didn't do anything. She wanted to do everything herself. The hair, the dress, and the makeup. She refused to have me do anything. Her door has been locked every since you are left. She is so independent. I will tell you that Lucifer could not have chosen a better partner."

I smiled, at her response. I was independent and just because I'm getting married in less than an hour, does not mean that I am going to give up my independence.

The reason I would not let Zaphara do my makeup was that this is my big day. I'm the one who is getting married to a guy that I love. When I walk down the aisle I want him to see the real me, not my super made-up face and perfect hair.

Don't get me wrong, Zaphara is an amazing beautician but I want this day to be about me, not her.

My makeup was very simple. All I had on was mascara and a bit of lipstick. My hair, I curled, twisting a large portion of my hair into a bun. The rest, I let hang down.

My dress wasn't too fancy, but it wasn't too simple either. Even though Miss Lillie made it for me, I helped with the finishing touches. The top of the dress was very plain, with no straps. Elastic ran around my waist, which made the dress hug my hips. Below the waist, the dress flared out, and it stopped right at my ankles. As I said, the dress was very simple.

The thing I liked the most about the dress was the finishing touch, I had Miss Lillie add. Like my ball dress, I wanted color in my dress. So, from the waist down, I had her add grey to the dress, which she did. I wanted grey because it represented the fact that I am neither good or evil. Like me, the world is in a constant battle between the two, like everyone else. In a world where both exist, I believe that both can coexist, peacefully.

"I'm ready," I said, opening the door all the way. Zaphara turned to me and gasp.

"Hey, baby? We're ready. I'll see you in a bit," she told Miss Lillie and then hung up. "You look amazing!"

I smiled at her and walked past her. "I know," I said as I headed to Lucifer's study. The portal was in his study.

Zpahara walked next to me and activated the portal. "Ready?" she asked me.

I nodded. "It's time for me to get married."

As soon as we reached Earth, I took a deep breath. It has been about a month since I have had any fresh air. I really have missed being on Earth.

We had to walk about half a mile to get to the ceremony. As soon as we neared the field, I chose to get married at, Zaphara called her wife and told her to start the music.

"Okay, this is where I leave you," Zaphara gave me a hug, and kissed my cheek. "I love you."

"I love you too. Thank you so much for everything you have done," I said, as I hugged her back. I watched as she walked away.

"Okay," I said, taking a deep breath. "Let's do this." I looked at the guy at the piano and nodded. Smiling at me, he started the music.

I took one step on the white carpet, when I heard a voice behind me, say my name.

I spun around to see Micheal stand behind me. "You came!"

"Of course! Why would I miss one of the most important days of your life? But before I walk you down the aisle, I must ask you 'Are you sure you want to do this because you don't have to'."

I smiled at him. "Of course, I want to do this and I want you to be there for me."

"I will be there for you, every step if the way. Now, it's time to get you married."

I grabbed Micheal's arm and we walked down the aisle. With each step I took, my heart seemed to beat faster.

Was this really happening? Am I making the right choice? Is this a dream? What if I'm making a bad choice?

All of a sudden, all the questions I had, disappeared because right in front of me stood my future.

"You look...I can't even find the world to describe you," Lucifer whispered, as I stepped up to the altar.

"Thank you," I whispered. "You look very handsome."

"Now for your vows," Miss Lillie announced as the ring bearer gave us the rings so we were to give to each other.

We both took a deep breath, as we turned to each other. I spoke first.

"Lucifer, I will admit, the first time I saw I hated you. You interrupted me when I was solving a math problem in Mr. Johnson's class. From that first day, I wanted to punch you in the face." I paused as everyone laughed. Lucifer let out a little chuckle. "I mean, you kept popping up every time I turned my back. Don't get me wrong, I was grateful for all the times you were there when I needed help but then there were those times I didn't.

"But as we spent more time together, I realized that fate or not, destiny or not, you were the one that I wanted fighting by my side, no matter what. When it comes down to it, you will always be there for me and I will always be there for you.

"I never want to spend another day without you. I love you, Lucifer. You truly are my Demonic Guardian Angel."

A few people from the crowd, clapped as others sniffled. Lucifer held his finger up to me and smiled. I slipped his ring on, smiling at him.

"Raven," Lucifer started. "From the moment I saw you, so many, many, many years ago...man that sounds creepy," he said, with a smiled. The crowd laughed and so did I. He cleared his throat and began again. "From the moment I saw you, I knew that you were perfect. I could see that your soul was so pure, so full of innocence that it was blinding. I wanted nothing more than to be there for you.

"I will admit, I watched you as you grew up. I know that you always thought you were alone, but trust me, you never really were alone. I was always there for you. I watched out for you like I promised your parents I would.

"When you chose to save both sides, you surprised me. I have never seen anyone so perfect, so fearless, so selfless as you.

"I know that I don't have a soul, but when you were taken from me, I felt like my soul was stolen from me. I didn't take time to rest, I didn't take time to eat, I didn't take time to do anything but find you. When I finally got you back, I was relieved. I knew then and there, I wanted you to be my wife.

When I am with you, I feel whole. You, Raven, are my soul. You are my everything. I will do anything to protect. I never want you to have a day where you are sad. I never want you to have a day where you feel alone. I love you Raven and as long as we live, I will keep loving you."

Lucifer motioned for my hand, and I smiled. I held my hand out to him, and he slipped the ring on my finger.

"You are so perfect, so beautiful so amazing. I will worship every breath you take. I will worship every step you take. I will do everything in my power to make you happy for you are my wife. You are my life. You are my Diabolic Angel."

(